Karma Unleashed

The Tales of Karma

Natasha Tynes

Contents

Prologue

K ARMA COULDN'T REMEMBER her first vision. She'd always had them.

Visions flashed before her uninvited, showing snippets of lives yet to be lived. They played like short Hollywood movies. She saw them everywhere—on her way to school, while playing with the neighbors, while seated on the bus, and while singing in the school's choir. They were all triggered by physical interaction: a mere touch, a handshake, a tug, or even a brush on someone else's hand. When they happened, she became oblivious to her surroundings. To the outside observer, she would appear to be staring into space, like someone high on an illegal drug. Sometimes, a dull headache would precede the visions and linger for a while after they vanished.

But which one of those visions was her first? Was it when she saw Auntie Wafa falling down the stairs of their apartment building, breaking her neck three days before it happened, or was it when she saw Bassam, the next-door neighbor with an arm cast, a week before he fell off his bicycle?

No, no, it might have been when she was seven years old, when she saw her neighbor, Arwa, on a plane, months before Arwa told her Karma was immigrating to the US from the city of Shifa in the Arab country of Bilaq, where they lived.

"I already know that," Karma told Arwa when she broke the news. They were eating Falafel sandwiches while sitting in white, plastic chairs in their apartment building's courtyard. It was a hot day, the sunlight bright in their eyes.

"Who told you?" said Arwa, squinting her eyes. "We just found out our papers were approved yesterday. Was it my brother Rami? He has such a big mouth!"

Karma took a deep breath and inhaled the scent of the jasmine flowers planted in a garden bed near the main gate of their apartment building. "No, it was not Rami. I just know things," said Karma, then bit into her sandwich as she revealed her secret to her childhood best friend.

Arwa rolled her eyes and tucked a strand of curly brown hair behind her ear. "You can be so silly sometimes," she said.

The two got silent as Karma watched their neighborhood cotton candy seller pass by their street. "Sha'r el banat, Sha'r el banat," yelled the boy, whose bright pink confection dangled from a wooden log hoisted behind his back.

No. Scratch that. Perhaps her first vision had happened when she was only five years old, when she saw her aunt chop her finger while cutting onions. Karma had tried to warn her. She had even gathered all the onions in her house and hid them in her mom's purse while they were visiting. Her aunt ended up losing part of her finger anyway. Karma's efforts to stop the incident had failed, and her mom's purse forever smelled like onions.

When Karma was young, she thought everyone had visions, believing the mystical was a human, mundane part of existence. Later, her mom explained to her that she had a wild mind with a wild imagination and that she was not normal but rather unwell.

Sometimes, her mom would curse the heavens above for what they had brought into her life.

"Ya Allah, why did you give me a daughter like this?" she would say, shaking her head.

"Ya Allah, you granted me one child and made her like this. Why Ya Allah, why?"

Karma would wish the floor to swallow her, erasing her forever.

"Don't go telling everyone about your crazy mind. Keep it to yourself," Karma's mom warned her as she prepared her school lunch, labneh with Zaatar spice inside a pita pocket. "We don't want people to start spreading rumors about you, saying you're crazy and that you'll never get married, ever!"

Her mom wiped the back of her hands on her dress, then looked Karma straight in the eyes. "Do you hear me? No one should know about this! No one would ever want you. You'll become an old spinster living with me and your dad," she said, tapping Karma's head with her index finger.

Of course, Karma didn't listen; instead, she told her friend, Rula, at the age of eight.

"I see things before they happen," said Karma as she sipped her banana-flavored milk during the school recess on a breezy September day. They were both sitting on a bench in the school's courtyard, watching their classmates run around. The concrete courtyard was bare, with no playground equipment, scattered toys, or any greenery. Aside from the worn-out benches, the yard was just an empty, open space for kids to run wild.

"What do you mean?" asked Rula, cocking her head.

Karma remembered her mom's warning. "Sometimes, I see things before they happen to people before they know it themselves. Sometimes, they're good things. Sometimes, they're bad things," she said, her eyes welling with tears.

Rula grabbed a cucumber from her lunchbox and took a bite. "How do you see them?" she asked while chewing.

Karma rested her arms in her lap. She quickly wiped a tear from her cheek, hoping Rula hadn't noticed. "In my head, they flash before me like a movie."

"Really? When? Can you see something about me?" asked Rula, voice loud with excitement.

Karma shrugged. "I don't know. I think it happens when I'm close to people. When I touch them."

"Touch me now. Please? I want to know what you see?" Rula closed her eyes.

Karma looked at her best friend, a light breeze ruffling her straight brown hair. "Not today. I don't think I can right now."

Rula insisted, "Come on, do it quickly. Before we head back to class!"

Karma grabbed Rula's right arm. She closed her hazel eyes for two minutes. When she opened them, she let out a big sigh. "Nothing. It doesn't happen every time. I don't know why."

"You're lying," said Rula, shaking her head. "I knew you were lying."

Karma felt the blood surge through her veins. "No, I'm not. I told you it doesn't happen to everyone I touch all the time."

Thankfully.

Rula stuck out her tongue. "Liar. My mom already warned me against playing with you. She said you and your family are strange and that we should keep our distance." She stood up, wiped the cucumber crumbs off her gray school apron, and walked away, leaving Karma alone on the bench.

As time passed, Karma realized her secret, terrified those who learned about it, making them run away. It was a supernatural concept beyond their comprehension, like when she was 15 and warned her classmate Joumana that her father would lose his leg in a car accident, forcing him into a wheelchair forever.

Joumana hadn't believed her. Instead, she said, "Be'id el Shar." (May God keep evil away.)

When Karma's vision proved true, Joumana came knocking on Karma's door. "You are Satan's daughter," Joumana yelled as soon as Karma opened the door.

Karma felt the sting of the insult, and then a feeling of dread crept in. "What happened?" asked Karma, her lips trembling.

"You cursed my dad! He's a cripple now because of you!"

I did try to warn her. Can I be forgiven? "I'm so sorry," Karma said, tears starting to fall down her cheeks.

"Stay away from me and my family. You'll only bring evil!"

Karma's mom was right. She had a crazy mind. She had to keep it to herself.

Her visions came and went. Sometimes, she ignored them, and other times, she acted on them. Occasionally, her visions would cause her headaches that her mom would cure with sage and chamomile tea.

When Karma was 17 and Samir, the convenience store owner on the street behind their building, brushed against her hand as he handed her change, an image flashed of him pumping gas in his car, somewhere foreign, away from Bilaq. Was it Europe or America? The few people around him had Western looks, blonde hair, and fair complexions. He was clean-shaven. His well-groomed mustache was gone. Where was he? There was greenery everywhere, and the gas station overlooked a mountain on the horizon.

She shook her head to ground herself back to where she was. She took a deep breath and looked at the store owner. "Ammo Samir, how are you?" she asked him.

"I'm good. How are you, ya bint?" (Little girl.) He always called her "little girl."

She wanted to find a way to tell him about the vision. She had to think fast. "Things are hard these days. My dad says no one has money. He dreams of leaving for America someday!"

"Ah, isn't that everyone's dream?" he said as he bagged her groceries. "My brother in Alabama is trying to convince me to move there. He even helped me apply for immigration. Who knows when it will happen?"

Karma smiled. "It will happen, inshallah." She was happy with this vision; Samir's dream was going to come true.

Sometimes, her visions terrified her, giving her nightmares, like when she was a senior in high school and saw her favorite teacher, Ms. Lilly, in a hospital bed. Her eyes were closed, and she looked frail, like a skeleton. Two IVs stuck out of her arm, and she had a tube in her mouth. Two young men and a young woman gathered around her. Her children, maybe? Was she dying? What would happen to her?

Would I ruin her life if I told her what the future holds? Would she believe me? Would she discipline me? Would she think I'm crazy?

She never told Ms. Lily about her vision, never looking into her eyes again after that day. Ten years later, Miss Lily died of ovarian cancer.

Karma sometimes stayed up at night, thinking and overthinking. Why was she different? Why did touch trigger her visions? Why did it happen with some people but not with others?

When she grew tired of tossing and turning, she would go to her parents' bedroom. Her mom would let her sleep beside her as her dad would sleep soundly, snoring at the far end of their spacious, wooden king-size bed, its frame adorned with irregular polygons that Karma liked to stare at to lull herself to sleep.

"Stop overthinking things, Karma," her mom would say, caressing her hair. "If you continue like this, you'll age quickly. Wrinkles will appear overnight, and then you'll never get married."

Karma knew her mom was right. Her visions were venomous, slowly poisoning her body and soul. Even the happy ones were evil because she was not supposed to see the future; no one was supposed to see the future except for God or the devil. God had made her that way, part human, part devil, she would think to herself, she recalled some of her most recent visions.

Every vision left a scar on her and changed her forever. She wished she were not the way she was. She would sigh and try to go to sleep, but she couldn't.

She wished her family would attend church, just like all other Christian families, comprising 5% in the predominantly Muslim country of Bilaq. Her family was a minority. She was a minority, a pariah. A pariah within a pariah, within a pariah.

Maybe being in a church close to God would heal her and exorcise the devil out of her, but her mother was adamant about not going to church.

"The incense at the church gives me an allergy," she would say. "And the priests are always cranky, and I don't need more drama in my life."

Her dad never objected to his wife's aversion to the church and went along with whatever she wanted. Her dad, her baba, was always like this—a peacemaker who wanted his girls to be happy.

If they ever got invited to weddings, funerals, or baptisms, her mother would stay outside the church by the front gate. She wanted to be seen, for her relatives to know that she had done her societal duty, but going inside gave her "heart palpitations," she claimed. "It's the incense. I can't stand it."

The incense is a hallmark of Greek Orthodox churches, where many Arab Christians pray.

Maybe I should go to church without my mother knowing; Karma would think late at night when she couldn't sleep. "Maybe God would accept me and cure me of this evil. Perhaps God is just testing me like he tested Job with the death of his children and leprosy, and all of that.

Her mom would put her hand on her head. "Shhhh. Shut that mind of yours."

Chapter 1

B Y THE TIME Karma reached nineteen, she had learned how to suppress her visions.

Her mom had taught her a trick. Whenever a vision started to form, she would close her eyes and try to push the images out of her brain, replacing them with her own happy memories: a trip to the beach with her parents or the summer she spent with her cousin Salam, who was visiting from the US. Her happy memories eventually trumped the flashing images.

Happy memories were her weapon. She was done with those silly, scary visions. She wanted to be normal. She ached to be normal.

"See. It's all in your head," her mom would tell her. "Whenever these thoughts start to formulate, just push them away."

When she was in her senior year of college, her mom started sounding the alarm about marriage.

"You know you're not young. I pray every day for you to get married," her mom told her as they sat at the kitchen table, filling grape leaves with rice and lamb and rolling them to make waraq dawali.

Karma, as an only child, was responsible for fulfilling her parents' dreams of becoming grandparents.

"But, Mama, you know my issue! Who would want a wife like me?" she said, her eyes on the grape leaf she was rolling.

Her mom shook her head. "You stupid child! We won't tell anyone about your crazy dreams. What have I been saying all these years? Just keep that to yourself," she said as she stacked stuffed grape leaves in the bottom of a deep pan. "Everyone has secrets. Even married couples. There's nothing wrong with that."

Karma raised her eyebrows as she tilted her head backward. "Really? What are your secrets, Mama? What did you hide from Baba?"

Her mom smiled. "They would not be called secrets if I told you, would they?"

Karma wondered if her mom's secret was that she had boyfriends before Baba. She wondered if she was not a virgin on her wedding day and faked her virginity by splattering tomato juice on the bedsheets like all those loose girls everyone warned her about. Was her mom not the perfect wife she pretended to be?

Or maybe her mom had inherited a lot of her money from her dead parents and stashed it away, hiding it from Baba.

Her university years at Bilaq State University in Shifa were uneventful. She took the bus to school, attended all the required classes for her Business Administration degree, and studied at home. She earned an A+ in every course and graduated with an almost perfect GPA.

"You've always been smart," Baba told her. "I couldn't be prouder of you," he said and handed her a $50 bill as a gift. She flipped the American currency and gazed at the portrait of the bearded man on the front, along with a gigantic, beautiful white building with a dome, and wondered if she would get to visit that building one day.

Karma made some new friends here and there during her college days, but no one became too close. She was always wary of getting close to someone, of being vulnerable, and of opening up in a moment of weakness, revealing her secret to those who wouldn't keep it.

At 22, suitors started showing up at the house. Karma obeyed her mom's commands and mostly stayed quiet as she served them Turkish coffee with a side of barazeq sesame seed cookies. The suitors came with their mothers, always accompanied by them, who did all the talking.

As it was customary, Baba kept his distance and let the women handle the matchmaking business. Sometimes, he would sit in a chair by the kitchen table, hoping to catch snippets of the conversations taking place in the nearby living room. Karma knew her Baba wanted her to end up with a great, strong man who would treat her like a queen, but he didn't want to interfere with his wife's maneuvering. He would interfere when needed.

Karma was always willing to defer to her mother in the matchmaking process, but if a vision appeared as her fingers touched a prospective suitor while serving him coffee, she wouldn't suppress it. She needed to know what she was getting into. She had to protect her future.

When she felt a vision coming, which was usually preceded by tingling in her extremities and a slight headache, Karma would lower her head, fixing her gaze on her shoes. This way, she can focus on the image without being distracted. Bowing her head down signaled her timid nature to the watchful eyes of her suitors and their mothers, making her a more desirable commodity: pure, virgin, untouched, as good as new.

In one vision, she saw a suitor in a prison cell, head shaven, armed crossed, pacing back and forth as other cellmates yelled at him, "Sit down, you crazy man!"

What kind of crime will he commit? What if he becomes a murderer? A wife butcher?

She turned him down.

In another vision, she saw a suitor nursing a whiskey bottle while sitting alone on a bed in a dark room. He was sobbing like a child. She turned him down, too.

I need a strong man.

She saw another suitor in a hospital bed with tubes coming out of his mouth. Two young men were standing by his bed. "He has suffered a lot," said one of the men as he looked down at the suitor in the bed. He sighed and then wiped a tear from the side of his face.

She felt bad for turning him down, but she didn't want to be the caregiver all her life.

When Jamal showed up with his mom at her parents' house, Karma was intrigued, mainly because no visions came to her when she touched him while serving him coffee. He's mysterious. I like that.

His mom, though, was another story. She was a heavyset, loud woman adorned with a stack of gold bracelets, heavy gold earrings, layered gold necklaces, and a generous application of makeup.

When Karma kissed her on both cheeks, as was customary, a powerful vision flashed before her eyes so quickly that Karma didn't have time to prepare herself to obscure it. She flinched and took a step back. A sniff of jasmine filled her nostrils as she saw Jamal's mom dancing happily at what looked like a wedding reception. She was wearing a long, dark blue dress and waving her arms, tapping her feet as she swayed to Arabic pop music while her golden bracelets clicked together, making a chiming noise that could still be heard amid the loud music. She looked ecstatic. Whose wedding was this, her son's wedding? Was it Karma and Jamal's wedding?

Karma's mom quickly recognized the look on her daughter's face and subtly shook her head, a signal to Karma to control her vision before she made a scene in front of her suitors.

Karma's mom had already gathered as much information as possible about Jamal from friends of friends, cousins, and cousins of cousins, and briefed Karma on it. Jamal, who was born in the city of Shifa in Bilaq but had moved to the United States when he was ten, had come to the country looking for a wife from his hometown. Acquaintances had told his mom about Karma, describing her as a decent girl from a good family, pretty and studious, an excellent homemaker who mostly kept to herself. They said that Karma had never strayed and told her about her stellar reputation. A virgin, for sure. Never been touched. No question about that.

Karma wondered if Jamal's mom had ever asked her elementary school classmates about her. What would they have said? That she claimed to have visions of the future and was mentally ill? Would Jamal's mom have brushed it off as a child's fantasy?

Jamal was tall with broad shoulders, with slicked-back, pitch-black hair and light brown eyes. He was clean-shaven and had a baby face. When they visited, his mom did all the talking while he stayed quiet. Occasionally, he would look at Karma and smile. When Karma first laid eyes on him, she thought he was handsome and felt butterflies in her stomach, a fuzzy feeling she had never experienced before.

Jamal's mom boasted to Karma's parents about Jamal's brilliance. "He was always an A+ student and received numerous scholarships," she said. "He was accepted into a top medical school, one of the best in the US, and now he's a heart surgeon."

Jamal's Arabic was not perfect by any means. Still, he would occasionally use Arabic words here and there. Karma would just smile when she heard his Americanized pronunciation of Arabic words, such as "kawa" for coffee instead of "gahwa." Karma's English was decent, thanks to the private school her parents had enrolled her in. She was their only child, after all.

Karma's mom talked about Karma as if she weren't sitting right there. She told them about her accomplishments, such as her excellent English skills, which had been developed through extensive schooling, and her recent graduation from business school. She also mentioned that Karma had always dreamed of having a family, excelled at cooking, and aspired to start her own restaurant someday.

"You should just try her magloubeh," Karma's mom said. "I can't even match it. When she makes it, all our neighbors ask for a serving."

"Mashallah!" Jamal's mom responded.

"She has a secret mix of spices that she refuses to share with anyone, not even me!" said Karma's mom.

Jamal's mom smiled. "You must share it with your mother-in-law." Karma blushed. Mother-in-law? Is this really happening?

"We can help her start her restaurant," said Jamal's mom. "But maybe after the children come and after they're grown up a bit."

"Of course! Karma loves children," said her mom. "She's healthy and has hardly been to a doctor. Her periods come right on time. She'll be pregnant in no time, inshallah."

Karma looked at Jamal, who stared at the floor. Was he as embarrassed by this discussion as she was? From the slight blush on his face, she gathered that all the talk about periods and pregnancies made him uncomfortable.

She liked him.

KARMA AND JAMAL got engaged a week after the visit. During their courtship, they went out to eat on three separate occasions.

Jamal opened up when they were alone, asking her about her childhood, her hobbies, and her friends.

"I can't wait to taste your food," he said, taking a bite of the steak he had ordered for dinner.

She blushed and took a bite of her spaghetti.

It was Karma's first time at that restaurant, known for its high-quality food and expensive Western dishes.

"So, how did you learn how to cook that well?" he asked.

"The internet," she said.

He took a sip of water. "Really? Tell me more."

"I watch YouTube and Instagram videos all the time," she said slowly, hoping that her accent was not too thick for him to understand. "There is everything out there. All the Arabic food I like. Magloubeh, Mansaf, Mujaddara. All of it. They show you everything step by step."

"Wow, maybe you can start your own YouTube channel one day. I'd be happy to help set it up for you."

She smiled. "Insha'Allah," she said, her heart expanding with happiness.

He's so supportive, she thought. A Bilaqi-born husband would have made fun of her.

Another dinner was followed by a movie in which he held her hand in the dark, and she felt she couldn't breathe from both excitement and embarrassment. Everything about him exhilarated her. She even loved that they looked alike—the same dark brown hair, hazel eyes, and olive complexion.

They got married a year later after her fiancée visa arrived. The church service was held at a Greek Orthodox church and attended by close family members. Karma's mom was agitated the whole time, making Karma wonder if her mom was really having heart palpitations or if she hated going to church for some unknown reason.

KARMA'S WEDDING CEREMONY was elaborate, attended by first, second, and third cousins, friends, and neighbors. Everyone danced to loud Arabic music well past midnight at a banquet hall at a five-star hotel in Bilaq. Jamal gave her diamond earrings, a diamond bracelet, and a diamond necklace as a wedding gift, and Karma couldn't believe her luck, her fortune. He is handsome, kind, and rich. What more could she ask for?

"Don't ever wear them," her mom told her. "You would lose them. Put them in a safe. You might need them when things get tough. In life, you can't guarantee things."

What would happen? Thought Karma.

Would we ever get divorced? No, I would have known by now if there were red flags. My mom is just being a paranoid, overprotective mom. But would Jamal leave me if he discovered my secret?

THEY SPENT THEIR wedding night at a hotel by the sea south of Bilaq. In their hotel room, she nervously slipped into the special, white satin lingerie her mom had packed for her. She'd heard horror stories of pain and blood during a woman's first time. She'd even heard of women who had to spend their wedding night in the hospital because their husbands were too eager, too rough. But Jamal was kind and gentle, and he made sure she enjoyed every minute of the act until the moment of the ultimate submission when she became a woman. There was pain and blood, as expected, but the experience was far more enjoyable than she had imagined. And the best part: no visions came to her, despite all that touching and more.

Six months after the wedding, Karma was more than ready to move to the United States to escape her mom and her life in Bilaq. She needed a change. She was eager to be a wife and a mom. She was prepared to embrace the American life she admired, thanks to the countless hours she'd spent watching American entertainment. She wanted a single-family home instead of the dingy apartment she'd lived in her entire life. She yearned for the greenery of a beautiful, quiet suburban neighborhood. She wanted to stroll into big malls and have significant food portions. She wanted the big SUV and the long highways. She wanted to wear whatever she wanted: shorts, sleeveless tops, and flip-flops, like the suburban women she'd seen online. She wanted to show her skin without being given weird looks, or getting catcalled or, in some instances, pinched.

She even wanted to go to Walmart and Costco, places she'd only heard of in American sitcoms.

She wanted it all. The entire American dream.

At the very least, her version of the American Dream.

As she said goodbye at the airport, she promised her mother one more time, "I'll never tell Jamal about my visions. Never in a million years."

"You're a married woman now. You need to act like it," her mom said, tears welling up in her eyes.

A middle-aged, Western-looking woman dragging a heavy carry-on bag passed by them, brushing Karma's shoulder. Karma saw her at a bar drinking an alcoholic drink beside a man who had his hand on her thigh. She could see the lust emanating from both of their eyes.

Yes, she still gets visions. But she was on the cusp of the American dream, a life with a successful, handsome husband. She wouldn't risk any of that for the world. Jamal would never find out.

❋ ❋ ❋

KARMA'S MARRIED LIFE was everything she hoped for and more. Jamal was kind and hard-working. He worked long shifts at the hospital while she occupied herself with decorating the house and prepping meals. When Jamal was home, he was attentive and caring. He helped her with the housework, something she had never seen her own father do. On weekends, they took long walks in the nearby woods, where they exchanged stories about their childhood.

"I never fit in," he confided early in their marriage, squeezing her hand. "My looks, my parents speaking with their accented English, the spicy food I brought to school lunch, I always felt like an outsider."

Karma squeezed his hand back, reassuring him but also reassuring herself that it was safe to touch him without incident. "Really? That's surprising. You're just so American to me."

He chuckled. "I'm glad I fooled you. Looks can be deceiving, but I'm different—no point pretending otherwise. My name, for one. I always dreaded the roll call on the first day of school."

"But Jamal is such a normal name!" Karma exclaimed.

"You'd think so, but it's not James or Nick or Sam or any of the easy names I wished I had when I was a kid. Then there's the fact that I lived with my parents until I got married and that I kiss my mom's hand every time I see her." He brought Karma's hand to his mouth and pressed a kiss into her knuckles.

How did she get so lucky?

She felt a wave of joy travel across her body. "Honestly, babe. It's only with you that I feel like myself. I can't wait for us to have a family of our own soon. When that happens, this country will finally feel like home to me."

"We'll have a big family, inshallah," said Karma, her cheeks hurting from smiling. "I'll be happy with five children."

He jerked back playfully. "Five! I'm not paying college tuition for five children," said Jamal, laughing. "University is expensive here."

She touched his face tenderly, her fingers tracing the familiar contour, and smiled. "Don't worry. They will be brilliant, and they'll all get scholarships."

Two deer jumped in front of them, startling them, and then ran to the nearby creek.

She shivered. Jamal wrapped his arms around her to warm her up. She relaxed against him and reveled in her new life.

Also unexpected, Jamal showered her with gifts. Flowers, perfumes, jewelry, and chocolate. Like in a romantic movie, at least once a week, there was a surprise waiting for her. He would leave her presents around the house with a sweet note, such as a KitKat, her favorite treat, on the pillow. Fresh flowers were delivered to her door, and a velvet box with a pair of delicate silver earrings would appear in the car's passenger seat. She was relieved he didn't share his mother's taste for bold gold jewelry.

"You look so beautiful today," one of the notes said.

"Can't wait to make love to you tonight," another one said.

Such pampering was foreign to Karma, something she'd only seen in American movies. Her dad was kind to her mom, and Karma had very few memories of them fighting, but showering her with gifts was something that he didn't do. Maybe it was because they never had much money, or maybe because, if he'd done so, it'd make him look as if his wife controlled him. He would be mocked by neighbors and family members as unmanly and lacking testicles. Men in Bilaq are supposed to be tough, distant, and not slaves to their wives.

"How did you learn to be so romantic?" she asked when he handed her a dozen red flowers one evening when he returned home from work.

"I've been around," he said, coming behind her to kiss her neck.

"Tell me," she insisted.

"You don't want to know." She felt a sharp pang of jealousy twist in her gut, a cold, gnawing fear. Would he ever leave me if I didn't satisfy him?

Their lovemaking was primarily silent but passionate. He always checked on her during the act and made sure she was comfortable.

"Is this good for you?" he'd ask, looking into her eyes. She wanted to turn away from his gaze, embarrassed but excited, stunned that he cared so much. He never broke eye contact with her during their lovemaking and even made sure the light was on, something she hadn't been prepared for. "You're so beautiful. I want to watch you feel pleasure."

Karma found herself slowly falling in love with him. Mama was right yet again. Jamal is wonderful.

True to her word, she'd never shared her secret with him, no matter how close they got or how many gifts he left her. She didn't want to scare him away, to risk losing all she had with Jamal.

Strangely, she didn't have any visions when she was around him. Despite all the touching and lovemaking, nothing happened. He was just one of those people who never triggered visions in her. All those years, she still hadn't figured out what triggered the visions in some and not others. Was it their blood type, the color of their hair, or the color of their eyes?

Maybe she'd never know.

Settling into her new split-level house on Jasmine Drive with her new husband was exciting. She had a whole place to take care of and needed to learn a great deal about running an American household. She'd lived her entire life in a tiny apartment in the city of Shifa in Bilaq. Now that she had so much space, she spent her days decorating, gardening, and learning. She added new words to her vocabulary, such as perennials, compost, gutters, attic, and crawl space.

When she wanted a break from decorating and gardening, she would FaceTime her mom, thanks to the iPhones Jamal had gifted her whole family. They would chat for hours about her new life in the US and how happy she was.

"Jamal is a great husband," Karma bragged over the phone. She could see her mom in the living room, sitting on their worn-out brown fabric sofa. Part of her wanted to be back in that apartment, sitting next to her mom, but the other part felt completely content where she was.

"I told you," her mom said, smiling. "I knew that from the first time I saw him."

At five o'clock every afternoon, she would start dinner and wait for Jamal to come home. She made him all the dishes of her childhood: magloubeh (an upside-down rice dish), mujaddara (lentil and rice), musakhan (chicken with caramelized onions and sumac), and many, many more.

He always praised her. "Your food is even better than my mom's. Please don't tell her. She would disown me."

They laughed as he scooped a dollop of plain yogurt and poured it over both their rice dishes.

Some nights, he would stay late if there was an emergency at the hospital, so she would eat alone and then watch Netflix shows. She loved crime shows, especially those that happened in wealthy suburbs.

How do these well-to-do people who had everything they wanted end up messing up their lives so badly? She couldn't stop watching. One murder after the other. One tragedy after the other. What's wrong with these people?

She was blown away by the fact that these murders were discussed so openly on TV. That the victims and sometimes the murderer were given the chance to tell their side of the story. She was also stunned by how the American judicial system functioned and how 12 ordinary citizens determined the fate of the defendant.

Sometimes, she would stay up late reading eBooks on her Kindle, another gift from Jamal. She had recently discovered erotic novels and read them secretly when Jamal was not around or when he was beside her, sleeping. When Jamal would ask her what she was reading, she would say romance novels, and he never asked her more. The scenes in those books thrilled her, and she surprised herself by waking Jamal up in the middle of the night because she felt an irresistible need to have him inside of her. He happily obliged.

She had questions like, How could authors write these novels? Did they try all these sex moves in real life? Didn't they have any shame? Had their mothers ever read their books? Nevertheless, she enjoyed them and wanted to read more. It was her dirty little secret.

The retired couple next door had brought her casseroles and flowers when she and Jamal first moved in, and occasionally, they gave her tomatoes from their gardens. They asked her to watch their house and water their plants while traveling. They exchanged house keys and included their names as emergency contacts on the forms. But despite the neighborly waves, they stopped short of being true friends.

She didn't know where or how to make friends in the suburbs, but maybe that was okay. She had enough to do around the house in addition to keeping up with all her favorite Netflix shows.

But he seemed to feel otherwise. He was reading the news on his phone while she browsed Netflix on the TV mounted on the wall across from their bed.

"Maybe you can take a class or join a gym," suggested Jamal one night as they lay in bed. "Not like you need it. You're gorgeous. Just to meet new people and make friends."

"The gym isn't really my thing," she said, staring at the TV. "Paying money to move my body? No thanks. I'd rather walk for free."

Jamal smiled and looked at her. "It's okay, babe. We can afford it."

She felt a point of pride that they didn't have to worry about money. But she still didn't like the idea. "Not for me."

He put his phone down on the bedside table and then turned his head towards her. "How about you volunteer? Maybe at our local shelter?" he said, placing his hand on her thigh.

Turning off the TV, she looked at him. "Volunteering? You mean... work for free? Really, Jamal?"

He rolled his eyes. "You know, there is nothing wrong with that, but I give up."

"Maybe I can get a job," she suggested. "I can work at a bookstore. I love books."

"Do you need to get a job?" said Jamal. "I work day and night so I can provide for you so that you won't need anything."

"I know, habibi. I thought maybe I could help with some of the bills."

"No, babe. It's not worth it," he said, shaking his head.

Karma felt herself getting angry. What is he saying? Was he turning into one of those Bilaqi-raised men who preferred their wives to stay home and take care of the house and the kids? "You know, I've never had a job before. I married you right after college. I guess part of me wants to get that experience."

Jamal tsked. "What experience? Work is overrated. Do you want to have a nasty, smelly boss, long shifts, and cranky customers? Why? Let me deal with this. You just be happy and pretty for me. That's all I need," he said, then took a lock of her wavy brown hair between his fingers and twirled it.

"You're right," she said, then covered herself with the down comforter and closed her eyes. Maybe he is really not that different from the Bilaqi men. She sighed silently.

He scooched next to her, his thigh touching her thigh, then kissed her on the cheek. "You smell nice," he said, slipping his hand between her legs.

Not now, she thought. She felt sore. They had already had sex that morning.

An image of her mom wagging her index finger and saying, "Never deprive your husband," flashed before her eyes.

By the time that image was gone, Jamal was already on top of her, his manhood finding its way in while his right hand twisted one of her nipples. She could smell his minty toothpaste as he moaned in her ear, thrusting in and out of her. "Please don't go to work and ruin that gorgeous body of yours."

"How would work ruin my body?" she asked, almost out of breath.

"You will get varicose veins from standing up all the time, and your beautiful skin will suffer from all the stress," he said between his moans.

She placed her arms around his neck, pushing him further inside her, and said, "I won't, habibi, I won't."

She thought about her mom when she unexpectedly felt her body convulse with pleasure as the first wave engulfed her, the second, and the third. She's right. Never deprive a man.

Jamal was insistent that she find friends, but Karma's isolation didn't bother her that much. After all, she was used to being alone. She was an only child, and she avoided making friends growing up. Getting close to people was risky; they could learn about her visions and run away, just as Rula had rudely done all those years ago.

She had her books, shows, and housework. Soon enough, she would have kids to raise, and her life would have a higher purpose.

ONE DAY, ALMOST half a year after she moved to the US, an older woman bumped into her at the library. Karma tried to stop the impending vision, but it forced its way in.

She saw the woman on the deck of a large ship, sipping drinks and chatting with three other women who all seemed to be enjoying their time as they gazed out at the ocean before them. Seagulls flew overhead.

It looks like this woman will soon go on a lovely cruise. Lucky her! I guess there is happiness after seventy.

She thought of her mother's aunt, Abla, who, at seventy, locked herself at home, refusing to leave the house because, as she told them, she was "waiting for death." She was in perfect health, but quickly deteriorated when she gave up on life. When she decided it was time to go, simply because she was old. Going on a cruise at seventy was not in the books for Aunt Abla.

At least her first vision in ages wasn't one of nightmares.

Chapter 2

DAYS TURNED INTO weeks, weeks into months, and when a year passed, Karma started to get antsy. The suburbs had lost their charm, and so had life in the United States. The streets were too quiet, the neighbors were boring, and the shops had nothing new to offer. She had already finished watching her favorite shows, and her sex life was predictable. The honeymoon was over. Life in the US was no longer as charming as it had been portrayed in the movies. It was mundane, a mediocre existence.

She wanted more, and no, she didn't want to volunteer like Jamal suggested. She wanted kids, but despite their regular lovemaking, her period came every month, signaling her empty womb—her failure to achieve her purpose in life.

Jamal's mom was also getting antsy.

"What's going on?" she asked Karma on the day when she came to visit. They were both sitting on the front porch, sipping hot tea. Her gold earrings caught the light, blinding Karma. "Why are you not pregnant yet?"

"We are not rushing," Karma lied. What else could she say? That she was afraid she couldn't bear children?

"Really? What are you doing? Is he ejaculating outside?"

Oh, God! Did Jamal's mother really just use the word ejaculation?

"Yep," said Karma more calmly than she felt, taking a sip from her tea.

But she couldn't help but worry whether both her mind and her womb were deformed.

At night, Karma would rub her belly and wait for a vision, hoping to see herself pregnant, nursing a child, or swinging a toddler at a playground. Nothing came. No visions appeared. Was her future childless? Could she ever bear to live with that scary thought?

Would she consider other options like adoption or surrogacy? No, no! She wanted to experience pregnancy, natural childbirth, and breastfeeding. She wanted to experience it all.

Karma knew she would be a great mother. She had always loved kids and sometimes preferred their company over that of the adults. The children were pure and never judged her for her condition. She enjoyed playing with her younger cousins and her friends' younger siblings. She adored babies and loved to smell their heads. She was always curious to see if they would provide her with visions, and when they did, they were mostly positive: images of them on a playground or splashing in a pool. Karma was convinced there was a reason God gave women breasts, a womb, and round hips. Women were created to bear and feed children with their bodies. Women were never meant to be childless.

She thought about her mother and her struggles to have a second child. She remembered her mother talking about her issues to her friends. She remembered going with her mother to the doctor several times.

"Not sure there's anything we can do," Dr. Fawaz had told her mother at the end of her nine-year-old daughter's appointment.

She remembered seeing her mom cry as they sat in the backseat of a hot cab with a smoking driver and windows that wouldn't roll down.

She remembered her mom's joy when she got pregnant a few months after the doctor's visit and her devastation afterward.

"I just miscarried," her mom had told her between tears. "I just lost my baby."

Did she have her mom's infertility issues? Was that the reason she couldn't conceive? She panicked.

"Don't worry, sweetheart," Jamal told her a few days after her conversation with his mother as they were getting ready for bed. "We'll figure it out. There are a lot of great doctors here. We'll get checked out next week. I know a great doctor. Things will be okay."

He hugged her and wiped the tears streaming down her face with his thumb.

"I love you. We'll have a child soon. I'm sure of that," he said, pressing his forehead to hers. "Doctors are performing miracles these days, and medicine has advanced beyond our imagination."

Yes. He was a doctor, and he'd know these things. She hugged him tightly, not wanting to let him go. Sometimes, she wondered if he wanted children as much as she did, or if he was okay with being a childless couple forever. She wondered if his life in the US made him accepting of the idea of childless women—an oxymoron. Women should never be without children.

When their fertility tests came back as "undetermined," Karma shut herself in her room.

"I can't imagine my life without kids," she said, her voice breaking between sobs. "Remember when I said I wanted five children? I was serious. Now I can't even have one! Don't you see the irony here?"

"Sweetheart, who said we couldn't have kids? There are lots of fertility treatments out there." He tried to soothe her, but she felt like a failure.

"I'm so scared. So, so scared of all this fertility stuff—the tests, the needles, all of that. What if I go through all of this but still can't have a child of my own? How cruel is that?"

"Shh, shh. Don't talk like that. There are so many paths to explore. It'll happen to us. I promise you." He caressed her hair, then gave her a long kiss. "You know what, in the meantime, why don't we start thinking about your restaurant? Remember, that was your dream? We can start looking for a location and investors, then hire a chef. You can recreate all your wonderful Arabic dishes, and you don't have to do much. You can hire a manager, and you make decisions. This way, your time will be flexible."

She pulled away from him. "Not now, Jamal. I'm not ready," she said, her voice escalating. "Stop trying to distract me from what I really want."

He backed up, hands held up like a criminal on one of the cop shows she liked. "Okay, okay, easy. No need to yell at me."

She crossed her arms in front of her chest. "I'm not yelling. I'm just upset."

"Fucking, hell, Karma!" he shouted. "I give you everything. Stop whining like a spoiled brat!" He got off the bed and left the bedroom, slamming the door behind him.

A sob traveled up her chest and croaked out of her throat. Karma was shocked by his outburst. She had never seen him angry like that. All her life, no one had ever shouted at her. Not even her dad, who mostly kept to himself and let his mom run the house affairs.

For once, she wished she could see a vision when she touched Jamal.

Karma slipped under the covers. She wanted to disappear, to cease to exist. She looked outside the window. It was pitch black and gloomy. The suburbs are no place to experience joy. The only sound she could hear was the chirping of the crickets and a faint dog bark. Her Apple Watch, a gift from Jamal on their one-month anniversary, said it was eleven o'clock. It was six in the morning in Bilaq. Too early, but she didn't care.

She called her mom on FaceTime.

"You mean he just shouted?" her mom asked.

Shouting was an exaggeration, perhaps. But he had raised his voice. And his words were harsh. "He's never talked like that to me before."

She could hear her mom snicker. "Come on, Karma. Men get angry and yell all the time. That's why they're men. Would you rather have him cry all day like a woman?"

"Of course not! It's just... I've never seen him like this." Leave it to her mom to be less than understanding.

Her mom raised her voice slightly. "Did he hit you?"

Karma was taken aback. "What? Definitely not!"

Her mom sighed. "Then, what's the issue?"

"He has never done that before, and you know yelling can be traumatizing, too."

Karma could see her mom's eyebrows as they drew together. "Listen, habibti; men get worse by age. Their tolerance decreases, so brace yourself. We just have to tolerate them. God made us more patient. That's why we are the ones to bear children."

Karma sighed. Maybe Mr. Perfect American Husband had a flaw after all. In the grand scheme of things, she was lucky. Luckier than most women.

"You're right. I just have to tolerate him."

Karma went to bed early that night, thinking about what her mom had told her.

Women are more patient.

THE NEXT DAY, Jamal came home from work in a great mood. "Come outside," he said cheerfully as he walked in the door.

She cocked her head. "Why?"

"I have a surprise for you. It's in the car."

She walked with him to their asphalt driveway, where their black Honda SUV was parked. He opened the back door, and there, sitting quietly in the back seat, was a black puppy.

"Thought he would keep you company," said Jamal, smiling. "I'm sorry we bickered last night. I know you're stressed about fertility treatments. Maybe a puppy will help for now."

Karma looked at the puppy and didn't know how to feel. She had never owned a dog before. What was she supposed to do with it?

Jamal touched her back, nudging her closer to the panting dog. "He's a male lab. What do you think of the name Baladi?"

Karma climbed into the car. The dog whimpered and looked at her with sparkling eyes as he wagged his tail. She sat beside him, put her hand on his back, and petted him. As soon as she did that, a vision started to form in her head. She was about to begin suppressing it by replacing it with good memories, but then, without giving it a second thought, she let go. She was so exhausted and depressed that she let her guard down and let the actual vision take over her mind. She saw Baladi running off-leash in a vast green field and heard someone call his name. Baladi turned around and ran back to his owner, who petted him and gave him treats.

The pet was happy.

The owner was happy.

The owner was her.

It was the first time she had seen herself in a vision.

"I like the name Baladi," she told Jamal, smiling.

Baladi—Arabic for "my home."

Chapter 3

KARMA'S LIFE TOOK a turn when she started walking Baladi. Suddenly, she realized she'd become a member of an elite club of dog owners who stopped and chatted with each other about their dogs.

"What a cute pup," the blonde woman who lived around the corner gushed. "A lab?"

"Yes, a pure lab," Karma responded. She was proud that Baladi was purebred, having been purchased from a breeder for $4,000 just to make her happy. That he was from an upper-class breed meant he could compete in dog competitions, unlike mutts from the pound.

"Where did you have him trained? He's very well-behaved," the owner of the collie mix down the street said.

"I trained him myself," she said proudly.

The owner of a German Shepherd wanted them to walk their dogs together, while the owner of an Irish Terrier asked for a playdate.

And then there was the Dalmatian woman, as Karma referred to her, who lived on the street behind Jasmine Drive. She walked her dog, Sunny, at least three times a day while dressed in a long-sleeved shirt with a Dalmatian print and black pants. She had several of those Dalmatian shirts, with a slight variation in the size of the dots, and she never walked her dog without wearing one. Maybe Karma needed to abandon all her colorful garments and stick to wearing black so she'd match Baladi. After all, Sunny and his owner always looked like a happy pair. She even had a stone statue of a Dalmatian dog in front of her house, positioned right underneath the main floor-to-ceiling window that overlooked the street.

"El Amreekan are majaneen—crazy," Karma's mom told her over the phone when she mentioned the Dalmatian woman. "It's hard for them to make human connections, so they focus on connections with animals. They are all majaneen."

Whenever the Dalmatian woman passed by Karma and Baladi in the street, she would simply nod and smile. No hellos or how-are-yous exchanged. Majaneen, indeed.

When Karma first met her neighbor, Veronica, and her dog, Rex, Veronica commented on how beautiful Baladi was. They were both standing on the sidewalk in front of Veronica's house, a tri-level, green abode at the corner of the street across from their house, with a manicured front yard and the greenest grass on their street.

"Rex doesn't get along well with dogs he doesn't know, but I'm surprised he and your dog get along really well," said Veronica, smiling as she petted her dog.

"Yeah, Baladi is very friendly," she said, looking at the large black dog wearing a head collar. "What kind of dog is Rex?"

Veronica put her hand in her jeans' side pocket, pulled out a treat, and gave it to her dog. "We're not quite sure, maybe a mix of German Shepherd and bulldog."

As she walked Baladi at least three times a day, Karma kept running into Veronica. One day, Veronica asked her to come over for a doggy playdate.

"A doggy playdate?" her mother scoffed. "Americans."

"How great!" Jamal gushed, practically patting himself on the back for his genius move. "I knew he'd help you make new friends."

He deserved the self-praise, she thought, as she had not cried in a full two days over her fertility issues.

A FEW WEEKS after their first meeting in front of Veronica's house, Karma and Veronica sat outside on the patio drinking a vodka seltzer on a mild summer day, a warm buzz creeping in after a few sips. It was her first time getting intoxicated, and she loved the feeling of letting go, of shedding her worries, of enjoying the moment.

She'd hardly drunk in Bilaq. She'd sometimes sipped on her dad's homemade wine and found it too bitter, but in the American suburbs, it was different; cocktails were part of the bonding experience of assimilating.

"Drink up," Veronica said, raising her glass. "God created alcohol for our good, for our survival."

"You think?" asked Karma, raising her eyebrows.

"Yes! Even Jesus turned water into wine. He knew we needed it for our sanity."

Karma smiled, then took a sip, remembering the story of Jesus at the wedding in Cana of Galilee that she learned at her private Christian school in Bilaq, a school attended mainly by the Bilaqi Christian minority. She thought of how alcohol was mostly an accepted commodity for Bilaq's Christian minority, who were the only ones allowed to open liquor stores and wouldn't be frowned upon if they consumed it at social occasions or in the privacy of their homes.

Veronica was vocal and funny, outspoken and direct. Karma related to her in a way she hadn't with others in the suburbs, who measured every single word that came out of their mouths.

From the corner of her eye, Karma noticed Veronica's vegetable garden tucked at the end of the yard with chicken wire surrounding it. "What are you growing?" she asked.

Veronica leaned back in her chair and lowered her baseball hat to protect her eyes from the sun. "Ah, this and that: tomatoes, cucumbers, squash, potatoes, and herbs."

Karma felt a pang of jealousy. "Nice. I should do that, too. I never had a vegetable garden. I've been trying to grow flowers, but I haven't been that successful."

"I can help you. Ask me anything. I love gardening," said Veronica, twirling her glass of vodka seltzer.

The pungent aroma of mint filled Karma's nostrils, and she felt nostalgic for her life in Bilaq. She remembered her dad serving her mint tea as they watched Al Jazeera together in the living room, lounging on their worn-out leather sofa. She recalled sipping cold mint lemonade in a coffee shop that overlooked a hill dotted with white brick houses, enjoying a cold summer breeze. At the same time, Arabic music played loudly through the café's stereo.

"Is it easy to plant mint?" Karma asked in a dreamy voice, careful not to break her trance.

"Oh yeah, it's the easiest thing," said Veronica. "It's like a weed. You plant it once, and it grows everywhere."

Karma's thoughts then drifted to the sweet smell of jasmine. She remembered walking through the neighborhood streets of Bilaq, passing by the lavish houses of the wealthy, each adorned with jasmine plants in their front yards. In Bilaq, it seemed every house and apartment building boasted a jasmine tree, their fragrant blossoms perfuming the air. To her, jasmine was more than a scent; it was the smell of home.

"What about jasmine? Can you help me plant some?"

"Jasmine isn't easy to grow here," said Veronica. "I found a plant by chance at the Korean store down the street, but yeah, otherwise, most things are easy to plant. I'll teach you some tricks, and since you live on Jasmine Drive, you have to grow some," she said, letting out a tipsy laugh.

Karma and Veronica fell silent, watching Baladi and Rex chase each other around the yard.

After a few drinks, Karma started opening up to Veronica, sharing stories about her childhood and how difficult it was for her to date men freely due to cultural restrictions. She shared her fantasies. "I've always wanted to go out on a date to the movie theater and share popcorn and Skittles with a boyfriend, just like in American romcoms," Karma said, slurring her words. "I wanted the boy to kiss me when he dropped me off in front of my house, just like in the movies."

"Oh, how sweet," said Veronica, smiling.

Karma rolled her eyes. "Of course, that never happened. The first and only guy who kissed me was Jamal, and that was after we got engaged."

"Are you fucking kidding me?" said Veronica, then took a big gulp from her drink. "That's a big risk! What if he was bad in bed? What would you have done then?" Veronica glanced at the dogs, who were both barking at a squirrel climbing the pine tree at the far end of the yard.

Karma got quiet, measuring her words. "I don't know. I would've just sucked it up, I guess, just like a good wife. But trust me, I don't have that problem now. Jamal is amazing in bed, and he wants sex like every day, or maybe every hour."

"Is that good or bad?" asked Veronica.

"I'm not sure," said Karma.

They both laughed.

Karma caught herself staring at Veronica's hands. Her skin was so fair, almost translucent. Was that normal to be so white? Had Veronica been born with such a complexion, or had she lost some pigmentation as she got older? Is that even healthy?

A distant sound of a lawn mower interrupted her thoughts. The lawn mower, the chirping of cicadas, and the blowing of leaves—all these sounds were foreign to her until she moved to the American suburbs. Now, they were all normal to her ears. Maybe she had assimilated after all.

"Marriage is not for me. I date them and leave them," said Veronica, then let out a loud laugh. "Stop, Rex, Stop! Stop biting Baladi's ear!" she shouted.

"Oh, what about your son's dad?" Karma asked. Veronica had mentioned a son a few times, as if he were just an accessory in her life, not the center of it, as he might have been if they had been living in Bilaq.

Veronica crossed her arms and let out a long sigh. "Oh, it was just a one-night stand thing. We never got married."

Karma blushed. Could she be friends with someone like that? What would her mother think? Maybe she should just leave Veronica's house now and never talk to her again? She couldn't wrap her head around women having kids out of wedlock and being so open about it. Apparently, in the States, nobody judged them. Nobody shunned them. Nobody killed them in the name of protecting the family's honor.

It must be nice. Veronica probably hadn't even tried to get pregnant, yet here she was, a mother, when that was all Karma wanted in the world.

A sadness washed over her for the first time since getting her puppy. "I have to go," she said abruptly as she stood up, wobbling a little from too much alcohol. "Baladi needs to nap. I can see he's getting cranky."

She stumbled back home, wiping tears from her face as Baladi led the way.

TRUE TO HER promise, Veronica showed up the next day with gardening tools. She started with Karma's front yard, weeding, digging, and planting some perennials she'd purchased from Home Depot.

"I also got you some mint," she said, handing her a small pot. "I'm still looking for jasmine. The Korean store is out of them. You might have to order it online."

Now and then, Veronica would bring her a new plant to add to her garden.

"Here you go," Veronica said one morning when she showed up unannounced at Karma's house. She handed her a long plant with green leaves. "This is called a Black-Eyed Susan. It's native to our state. It requires little care. Just water it every day, and it'll grow every summer. One of my favorite plants."

Karma's days were becoming busy and enjoyable. She hardly thought about her issues—the infertility, the loneliness, her visions. She felt normal and happy. When Karma was not spending time with Veronica, she focused on learning about raising her dog. She read articles on the American Kennel Club website and rewatched one YouTube dog training video after the other. In addition to teaching him how to sit and play catch, she also taught him how to shake hands and give high-fives. She put him on a rigid schedule, including three walks daily, three meals, and two snacks.

She spoiled her dog and spent a lot of money on toys and gear from Amazon. She loved the American notion of instant gratification, where anything she wished for would arrive at her doorstep in a day or two and sometimes even overnight. Boxes and more boxes came to her house—leashes, collars, treats, dog water bottles, chew toys, dog beds, and a dog pool. Jamal didn't seem to mind.

Baladi made a morning person out of her. She loved walking him early, watching the sunrise in the nearby woods, where she would listen to Fairuz's music on her AirPods and plan her day, which would usually include a dog playdate of some sort, making dinner, gardening, and doing the laundry.

The dog, the garden, and her new friendship with Veronica were giving her life.

One late summer day, Karma was sitting in Veronica's yard, enjoying the cool breeze and listening to her tell a story about kitchen remodeling and the issues she had with the contractors.

"The counter was a completely different color from the one I ordered, and they insisted I pay for it. I was like, no way, and threatened to sue them," said Veronica, spilling her drink as she waved her arms. "Of course, they replaced it the next day. Just mention a lawsuit, and they will come to you with their tail between their legs."

Karma nodded her head, feigning interest in the conversation. She was elsewhere, lost in a trance. The evening's gentle embrace and the tipsy warmth from the alcohol coursing through her veins made everything else seem distant and unimportant.

While Veronica went on and on about her kitchen remodeling, Karma found herself staring at Veronica's face, her light skin, her black hair, and the freckles on her cheeks. Freckles were a rare sight in Bilaq, so she kept staring at the dots scattered below Veronica's eyes and right about her cheeks. Small dots screaming for attention. What caused them? Why were they more prevalent in some races than others?

Her trance was interrupted by the arrival of Dominic, Veronica's teenage son.

"Come here, Dom," said Veronica. "Say hi to our neighbor, Mrs. Ibrahim," she said, slurring her words.

Mrs. Ibrahim! She was not used to being called that. It was a name associated with Jamal and his family. Why was this naming tradition still prevalent in the land of the free?

Karma stood up and said, "You can call me Karma."

Dom was handsome and tall, standing at approximately six feet. His long, black hair was tied up in a ponytail. His broad jaw and brown eyes were not a result of Veronica's genes. Did he take after his mystery father? A tight Under Armour shirt emphasized his toned abs.

He was precisely the guy her younger self would have daydreamed about dating and kissing by his car in front of her house.

Stop this thought—stop it! He's just a kid.

They shook hands. "Nice to meet you," he said, his voice slightly hoarse.

As soon as their hands touched, a vision began to form, taking Karma by surprise, and she was too distracted to suppress it.

Her heart skipped a beat.

Dom was hanging from a rope, his neck twisted, eyes bulging, and lips blue. He was alone in the room, wearing the very same Under Armor shirt he had on now.

She felt nauseous and dizzy. She placed her hand on her forehead and closed her eyes.

"Are you okay?" asked Veronica, tilting her head. "You don't look well."

"I think I had too much to drink," said Karma, who was swaying and struggling to hold herself steady.

"Dom, honey, why don't you go to your room?" said Veronica.

"Nice to meet you, Mrs. Ibrahim," he said, then disappeared inside the house.

No. Not Veronica's perfect son. Karma wanted to throw up. She had to get out of there.

"Do you need coffee or water?" asked Veronica.

Karma shook her head. "No, thank you. I just need to head home."

Veronica placed her hand on Karma's shoulder. "Do you want me to walk with you?"

"No, thank you. I'm okay. I'll text you when I get home. I promise."

She leashed Baladi and hurried back home. She took a tumble a few feet from her house, but she quickly picked herself up and dashed inside.

She skipped dinner and went upstairs to bed, telling Jamal the fertility medicines the doctor had prescribed were making her tired.

She browsed through Netflix shows, trying to distract herself from what she had seen earlier. That didn't work, so she picked up one of her latest romance books.

It can't be right. It was the alcohol causing me to imagine things. Terrible things. Maybe it is the mix of fertility drugs with alcohol. Nothing bad would happen to that handsome boy. He seemed perfectly fine. Healthy and happy. Good mother. Nice home.

That night, as Jamal tenderly made love to her, Karma's thoughts were of Dom.

Whatever he planned to do, she had to stop it.

Chapter 4

KARMA HAD INSOMNIA most of the night, tossing and turning while listening to Jamal's snoring.

How would she tell Veronica about what she saw? Would Veronica think she was crazy? Why would her handsome son, who had all America's advantages, kill himself? It didn't make any sense. He had everything: looks, health, money, a loving mother, a big house, and sexual freedom.

Morning came, and Karma dragged herself out of bed, going through the motions in a daze. When early afternoon came, Karma counted down the hours until she could reasonably go to bed and forget about her vision until Veronica invited her over for drinks and a doggy playdate.

Maybe this was her chance.

Karma showed up armed with a plan. "So, Veronica, I was wondering. Would Dom be interested in mowing our lawn? You know Jamal is always working, and I'm not good with this stuff. We'll pay him, of course."

"Oh? Really?" She tilted her head while twirling her cocktail. "That's a good idea. Let me ask him. He might be interested. He's not doing much this summer besides hanging out with his girlfriend."

Karma's heart jumped to her throat. "Oh? He has a girlfriend." What if the girlfriend breaks up with him, and that's why he kills himself?

"Yeah. Danielle. A lot of drama, this girl." Veronica rolled her eyes, then took a sip of her mojito.

Drama? That must be it. Danielle must end up breaking Dom's heart.

"So, you don't like her?" asked Karma.

Veronica sighed. "I don't know. There's just something about her. I'm not sure she's the best influence on him, you know?"

Karma leaned forward, her eyes narrowing in a focused gaze. "Hmmm. How so?"

Veronica picked at a hangnail. "She seems off. It's hard to explain, but she hardly smiles and seems up to something nefarious. I don't know; it's just a hunch."

Nefarious? Poor Veronica. Poor Dom.

"Do you think they're in love?" In American teen movies, teenagers always fall in love with someone their parents disapprove of.

Would Karma have dared to defy her parents' wish and marry someone her parents disapproved of? She doubted it. Her parents were her world. They always came first. No man was worth that big of a sacrifice.

Veronica shrugged. "I have no idea. Honestly, I don't know what he sees in her. It's as if she's put a spell on him or something," she said, her gaze drifting off as if searching for an answer in the distance.

"Young lovers," said Karma, smiling. "They tend to fall hard, and love is blind."

Karma was trying to be positive and drive away negative thoughts. After all, she had no idea when he would act on what she had seen in her vision. Maybe Danielle was good for him, and she could help him with his issues.

"I guess," said Veronica, staring into space.

LATER THAT NIGHT, when Karma and Jamal were in bed, Karma suggested they hire Dom to mow the lawn.

"I was going to suggest that," said Jamal. "These days, I hardly have time to sleep. I'd rather spend my weekends taking walks with you and Baladi. Who's Dom?"

Karma smiled. Jamal was really bad with names. It was endearing. "He's Veronica's son. A good kid. You'd like him."

Dom didn't know his father. Maybe he needed a good male role model. Jamal could provide that.

Jamal tightened his arm around Karma. "Who is Veronica again?"

Karma playfully slapped his chest. "Come on. You know, Veronica. Our neighbor, the friend I've been spending time with, and her dog."

He kissed the top of her head. "Oh yeah. That Veronica. Yeah, sure. We can hire her son. I'm okay with that. And I'm glad you finally made a friend. Without having to go to the gym!"

She nestled against Jamal, a big smile plastered on her face. Her plan was working.

* * *

THE FIRST TIME Dom came over, Karma watched him closely from her kitchen window. He wore khaki shorts and the same tight Under Armour T-shirt he had worn the first time she met him, with AirPods tucked into his ears. He seemed to know what he was doing as if he had mowed lawns hundreds of times before.

She chopped vegetables, mesmerized by his movements, hoping that by watching him intently, she would figure out what was bothering him. He seemed fine. She continued to visit Veronica daily, expecting to get a glimpse of Dom.

One day, when he showed up in the backyard with his girlfriend, Danielle, Baladi started barking nonstop. He growled, then positioned himself to lunge at Danielle. Wow. Maybe Veronica was right, and this girl is just a mess. Baladi was never aggressive with strangers.

"Stop it, Baladi," said Karma. "I'm so sorry. I'm not sure what's wrong with him today. He's usually very friendly."

Karma smiled nervously at Danielle, who was tall and skinny with fair skin and long, black hair that reached the middle of her back. She wore tight jeans that accentuated her toned body, a sleeveless red tank top, and red Converse shoes. She was gorgeous, resembling one of those Instagram influencers with millions of followers who only post pictures of themselves working out or drinking lattes with their names misspelled on the cup.

Danielle gave Karma a peculiar look as if she was sizing her up, figuring her out. Danielle crossed her arms, then chuckled while still looking at Karma. "You're exceptional, aren't you?" asked Danielle.

"I guess so," said Karma as beads of sweat formed on her forehead. What did Danielle mean? Was she suggesting something about Karma's heritage?

As Danielle and Dom headed inside, Karma inhaled, detecting something familiar—rosewater. The aroma was so strong that Karma felt a headache surfacing as her nose twitched.

What is Danielle doing with rosewater? Is she making a special Middle Eastern dessert, or is it for her perfume? Danielle thought of her favorite dessert, sweet cheese rolls, Halwaet El Jeben, that her mom used to make all the time. Her mother had once told her that rosewater brings all the flavor, as she taught her how to make it.

"I hope they're using protection," Veronica said, sipping her gin and tonic.

Karma blushed and wiped the sweat off her forehead with the back of her hand. Sixteen-year-olds having sex was not something she could wrap her head around. Did she even know what sex was at that age?

"Are you worried she'll get pregnant?" Karma felt liberated talking about sex openly and freely without being judged, shamed, or mocked.

"I sure hope not," said Veronica, twirling her glass. "They're both smart, and I'm sure they don't want to ruin their life at this age, but who knows with kids these days?"

"Yeah, I agree," said Karma, shaking her head. "I remember in Bilaq, our pastime was playing with glass marbles in the streets with the neighborhood kids."

Veronica's eyes softened. "I bet you were happier. You didn't have boyfriend troubles or romantic drama to distract you."

Karma grew silent for a moment. She was happier. She thought about Dom and his girlfriend. Maybe his girlfriend was pregnant and wanted to get rid of the baby. Maybe he wanted to keep it, as his mother had kept him? Perhaps she wanted to keep it, and he didn't? Or maybe he was scared and overwhelmed by the idea of becoming a father. But were any of these reasons to hang himself?

"Hey, are you okay?" Veronica asked. "You seem distracted."

Karma shook away her thoughts. "Yeah, yeah. I'm fine—just a lot on my mind. You know, with the IUI scheduled in a few weeks. I just can't handle another disappointment."

Veronica reached over and tapped her knee. "Oh, honey, I'm so sorry. It must be tough. Have you tried acupuncture? My friend swears by it. She got pregnant right after her first session."

Karma smiled at her friend. "Not yet, but you're right, I should try it. The nurse at the fertility clinic recommended it, too."

KARMA HAD TO see Dom every day to gain insight into his intentions. She followed him, memorized his routine, and learned his whereabouts. Every morning, she'd walk the dog and pass by Veronica's house. She quickly figured out that he worked three days a week at their local donut shop, a short walk from their gated community.

One day, she summoned the nerve to follow him to the shop. She tied Baladi to a tree and then went inside.

"Oh, hi, Dom," she said, smiling, doing her best to sound surprised.

Standing behind the counter in a white apron and chef's hat, Dom smiled back. "Hi, Mrs. Ibrahim."

"Your mother didn't tell me that you work here."

He picked up a cloth and wiped down the counter. "Yeah, I started about a week ago."

"How do you like it?"

He nodded and looked around. "I like it," he said.

"Are you happy?" she asked. Shit, was that too direct?

"Yeah. I'm happy here. Everyone is nice, and I need the money. You know, I can't keep asking my mom for money." He chuckled.

She nodded, smiling, "Yeah, of course."

"How can I help you, Mrs. Ibrahim?"

Karma paused. She had no idea what she wanted. "What do you suggest?"

"Hmm. Let me think." He turned his head and looked at the shelved donuts behind him. "Do you like glazed donuts?"

"Yes, I love them!" She had no idea what glazed donuts were, but she didn't want him to think she was an uneducated immigrant from a Third World country.

"Then, in this case, maybe you should get half a dozen."

"Yeah, I'll do that."

When she got home, she took one bite.

Too sweet.

She threw the whole box in the trash.

* * *

THE NEXT MORNING, she stopped by the donut shop again.

Dom smiled, waving his hand. "Mrs. Ibrahim, good to see you again."

Karma felt her heartbeat accelerate. "Good to see you too. I can't get enough of those glazed donuts." *I'm so stupid. I should have asked for bagels instead. I can't think clearly.*

"Glad to hear it. Maybe you need a dozen this time."

"Yeah. A dozen sounds like a good idea." *I really don't need a dozen. I'm losing my mind around this kid.*

"Here you go," he said, handing her a box of donuts. "I will see you tomorrow, then." He winked.

Karma's heart dropped. *Does he know what I'm up to? Maybe he thinks I'm stalking him? Perhaps he thinks I have a crush on him? Maybe he has visions, too?*

Stop it, Karma. Stop it. I need to stop going to the store.

She didn't.

Every day, she'd stop by the shop and buy donuts that'd end up in the trash, then walk the dog in the late evening and stop by his house to try to catch a glimpse of him through his bedroom window. Sometimes, she would see him sitting at his desk, typing on his computer. Once, he turned his head and saw her watching him from across the street. He waved and went back to typing. She could see a hint of a smile on his face as he typed.

He thinks I'm crazy. A crazy old lady who stalks teenagers.

Then she saw her. Danielle. She stood next to him as he typed. She was wearing what looked like a sports bra and had a drink in her hand. *A whisky, maybe? Or is that soda? Her hair was disheveled as if they had just done it. Too young. Too young for this. Sex at that age would mess with your head.*

Danielle turned her head and looked outside the window. She locked eyes with Karma, then rolled her own eyes as if she knew what was happening in Karma's head. How could she? Danielle walked to the window and rolled down the wood blinds.

Karma held her breath. She promised herself that night to stop that charade. She would stop watching him. She couldn't mess with that nutcase, Danielle.

She didn't stop.

She kept passing by his house at night. Sometimes, she would catch a glimpse of Danielle entering or leaving his home with him. Sometimes, she would see them walking down the street, his arm around her.

She failed to see the problem. What was bothering him? Why would he want to end his life?

One night, as Karma passed Veronica's house, she saw that Dom's room was lit again. He was alone this time. She sighed in relief. Then her body froze. Across the street, under a flickering lamppost, stood Danielle. Still as a statue. Smiling. Watching Karma. Karma blinked and rubbed her eyes. But when she looked again, Danielle was gone. *I'm losing my mind.*

When visiting Veronica for their daily dog playdate, she would be distracted trying to get a glimpse of Dom here and there.

"So, I've been thinking a lot about becoming a mom, and I'm a bit terrified," she said as they sat in their usual spot on the back porch.

Veronica got quiet for a bit, then took a sip from her drink. "It was hard in the beginning; then it got easier, then it got hard again." She laughed. "I guess it's hard. You know... your kids will always be part of you. Even when they are adults and leave the house, they'll eventually return to you. You will spend an entire lifetime worrying about them."

Karma took a sip of her drink. "How was he as a child?"

Veronica got a dreamy look in her eyes. "Hmm. He was lovely. So cute and cuddly. But a bad sleeper, though. He's still a bad sleeper."

"Do you think he's happy?"

"Yeah. I would hope so," she said. "He seems happy most of the time. Sometimes, he shuts himself in his room and doesn't talk to me for days, but you know, he's a teenager. They do that."

Karma's mother would never have tolerated her closing herself in her room all the time. Was he planning something? Or was this normal for American boys?

"Right. "Do you ever worry about him? Like something bad would happen to him? Maybe drugs or something, or maybe he would join a group of bad kids." Karma felt her stomach tighten. Have I revealed too much?

"I worry about him, but he is a good kid. I did my best raising him. I can't control the future. I just hope for the best."

WEEKS PASSED, AND Karma still hadn't figured out what was bothering him, if anything was bothering him in the first place. She continued stopping by the shop, picking up anything she could think of just to keep chatting with him: donuts, bagels, coffee, and even scones, despite not knowing what they were.

And when he came to her house, she deliberately brushed her hand against his whenever she served him a glass of homemade mint lemonade after he finished mowing the lawn, hoping the brief touch would spark a new vision, one that would give answers.

But nothing.

She couldn't see anything.

The vision must be wrong. Just a hallucination, thanks to a mix of alcohol and the heat.

However, her visions were always real, and they didn't always occur immediately.

And then, Dom didn't show up to mow as scheduled.

"Oh, he's a teen boy. Probably got tied up with his girlfriend," Jamal said, attaching Baladi to the leash. "Don't worry about it. He can come another day."

But Karma was worried. "He always shows up on time. If something came up, he'd call or text, find a way to reschedule." She texted him and called him, but no answer. She called Veronica and texted her—still nothing.

Did he do it?

Her heart beat fast, and her palms grew sweaty. Karma quickly grabbed the leash from Jamal. "I'll be right back."

He frowned. "Babe? Where are you going? I thought we were going to walk together."

"We will. I just need to check something first," she said, almost stuttering, as she was starting to feel nauseous.

Baladi knew where she wanted to go and started walking toward Veronica's house. When they got there, everything looked normal. Veronica's car was in the driveway, and music blared out from the kitchen window.

Karma let herself into the backyard and knocked on the glass backdoor that opened to the kitchen. Veronica stood by the sink, washing dishes and dancing along to "Shake It Off." Karma kept knocking until her friend finally turned around. The look on Veronica's face made her worry. It was a look of disgust.

Veronica opened the glass door. "Karma? What are you doing here?"

Oh God, what if he were in his room now? What if she was too late? "I'm here to check on Dom."

Veronica crossed her arms over her chest. Her energy was all wrong, not that of a friendly neighbor, drinking buddy, or best friend. "Of course you are!"

Karma recoiled. "What do you mean? Is he okay?"

"He's fine. My son is fine," she said, her lips pressed together.

Karma backed away from the door. "It's just he didn't show up to mow my lawn today."

Veronica gave her a mean smile. "That's right. He didn't show up because I don't want him at your house."

Her heart lodged itself in her throat. Why was Veronica acting like this? "What? Why?"

Veronica slowly shook her head. "You think I'm stupid? You think I don't know what's going on?"

Karma wrapped the end of Baladi's leash around her hand so tight that it started to cut off her blood supply. "What are you talking about?"

Veronica's voice cracked, and Karma could see tears welling in her eyes. "I don't know why it took me so long to figure it out. You're obsessed with my son. It's disgusting. I see how you look at him. I know you go to the donut store every day. I've seen you walking by our house late at night, peering at his window. Whenever you come here, you only ask about Dom, Dom, Dom. Well, you know what? I get it now. You're a perv, a fucking pedophile."

Bile burned Karma's throat. Veronica had it all wrong. "What? No, no, Veronica, you misunderstand. It's not like that. You know I'm happily married. Please, let me explain."

"There's nothing to explain. I've seen you ogling him. Dom, Dom! That's the only thing you talk about. And those night visits are so creepy and gross. All that sexual frustration in your country has obviously fucked you up." Veronica reached up to shut the sliding door.

Karma tried to think quickly, feeling stupid for not having seen that coming. The irony, she thought. I'm supposed to be the one who sees things coming. Telling Veronica the truth might be the only way. "Please, I'm trying to help him. You must listen to me. I think his life is in danger."

Veronica huffed a big breath in and out. "Stop. I don't want to see you ever again. Stay away from my son and me and get out of my house, you Arab creep."

Karma felt as though a deep knife had been lodged inside her heart. "Veronica!"

"Get out! Get the fuck out!" Veronica slid the door shut and then locked it.

Karma ran home and went straight to bed. Baladi cuddled with her as tears fell down her cheeks.

"Babe. Where were you? I thought we were going for a walk?" Jamal asked. He was seated on the sofa watching a baseball game on the TV placed above the fireplace.

Perhaps she was a creep, an Arab creep.

"I don't feel well. Hormones." She knew that even with Jamal being a doctor, he'd never want to discuss hormones with her.

The next day, determined to set things straight, she sent Veronica flowers and a fruit basket with the message: It's not what you think it is. Please let me explain. I value our friendship, and I would never do anything to hurt Dom. Love, Karma.

The flowers and the fruit were returned to her house untouched.

As weeks passed, Karma grew used to her life without Veronica.

She did everything possible to avoid her house as she walked Baladi. Still, it was hard, as Veronica's house was on the corner of Jasmine Drive and Ott Street on the way to the neighborhood woods where Baladi loved to walk. Every time she passed Veronica's house, Karma lifted her head high and prayed for no confrontation.

"Why did Dom stop mowing our lawn?" Jamal asked, almost three weeks after their friendship had fallen apart, looking out over the long grass.

"He's busy at the donut shop," Karma said, avoiding eye contact. She really hated to lie, especially to Jamal, of all people.

"Hmmm. Well, why haven't you been to Veronica's lately?" Jamal came up behind her and pulled her into a hug, kissing the back of her neck. "I like it when you come home happy and tipsy."

Karma leaned into his strong body. "She's just going through some stuff, and I'm giving her a break."

Jamal squeezed her tight. "Women and their drama!"

The next night, as she was busy frying okra to make bamya, she heard loud sirens increasing their intensity. Firetrucks? She ignored them at first and continued frying until more sirens followed, then some more. Baladi started barking nonstop.

She wiped the back of her hands on her jeans, slipped into her house slippers, and then went outside. A fire truck, an ambulance, and two police cars had gathered at the end of the corner house, the house on Jasmine Drive and Ott Street.

Veronica's house.

A chill ran down her spine.

She ran toward the commotion, joining the neighbors standing on the sidewalk in front of Veronica's place, all of them looking worried.

"What's going on?" Karma asked John, her neighbor from across the street.

"No idea," he said. "But it can't be good given the extent of the emergency response."

Karma knew it was Dom.

A few minutes later, an EMT rolled a gurney out of the house, a very pale Veronica trailing behind them. Dom's eyes were closed, and there was an oxygen mask around his face. She saw red marks around his neck. She gasped.

When Veronica's eyes locked with Karma's, she charged toward her. "It's you! It's all you! You did this to him! You messed up his head! You fucking cunt, you killed my son, you killed my son!"

Karma took a step back, speechless. Veronica pushed Karma with all her force, and Karma fell to the ground. John, the neighbor, rushed and got her up.

"What's going on?" asked John. "What did Karma do?"

"She killed my son! She did it!" she shouted.

Karma clenched her fists so hard she thought she heard her bones crack. "That's not true," responded Karma. "I was only worried about him."

"I think you should go home," John whispered kindly to Karma, using her arm to block her from approaching the gurney.

The EMTs ignored the commotion and pushed Dom into the ambulance.

Karma walked home in a daze and collapsed on the bed.

Jamal called her a few hours later. "I wanted you to know before you hear it from anyone else. Dom was brought in earlier today," he said. "He was in a coma."

"I know," said Karma. "I saw the ambulance."

Jamal got silent, and Karma could hear his heavy breathing over the phone. "I'm sorry, babe. He didn't make it."

Karma felt a knife stabbing at her heart as a sharp pain traveled through her. It took her some effort to let out a breath. She stayed silent as she heard some typing in the background.

"Babe, are you okay? I'm so sorry. I know you liked the kid."

"How did he die?" She already knew the answer, but she asked anyway.

"He hung himself."

Karma threw her phone at the wall across from her and then let out a scream. She went to the kitchen and stacked the dishes in the dishwasher. She asked Alexa to play a song by her favorite singer, Fairuz. As she loaded the dishwasher and pressed the start button, tears streamed down her face.

Poor Dom. Handsome, sweet Dom.

She stayed in bed for at least a week. She kept Baladi in his crate for most of the day until Jamal came home and took him for a walk. She spent her days watching Netflix and going in and out of sleep.

She checked her email and social media every few hours, then chatted with her mom on FaceTime, telling her about a neighborhood teenager who took his own life.

"What a tragedy!" said her mom. "I don't understand why people kill themselves when they already have everything. We have nothing here, but we are happy. We have each other."

The neighborhood listserv was filled with gossip and conspiracy theories. Some blamed Veronica, saying she ignored him; others blamed the girlfriend, saying she abused him. Fights erupted online—people shaming each other and blaming each other. The debate expanded into how popular culture glorifies suicide. Karma couldn't read anymore. She unsubscribed from the listserv but read every news article she could find. The local newspaper reported that Dom's classmates had organized a vigil for him. She scanned the pictures and read the interviews with the students. No photos of Danielle. No mention of her. Did she even attend the vigil?

Some girlfriend. Maybe Veronica's instincts had been right.

Karma could not stop blaming herself for what had happened. She needed to return to how she'd been before, avoiding touching people and using her technique to drive away visions.

She should have minded her business, just like her mom had told her. Her mom was right. Her mom was always right.

Now, she'd lost both Veronica and Dom.

AFTER WEEKS OF self-isolation, Karma broke down and told her mom everything. The friendship, the vision, the fight. The suicide.

Karma's mom listened but didn't speak. "Mama?" Karma saw her mother roll her eyes.

"Yes?" her mother said.

"Why are you so silent?"

"I'm just disappointed."

Karma sighed. "I know."

"Why did you let your crazy mind take over like this? You could have ruined your life."

Karma's voice cracked. "I was just weak. I drank alcohol and couldn't stop the vision. I slipped."

"Promise me not to drink alcohol ever again," she said, softening her voice. "You simply can't. You, of all people, can't handle it. Your mind goes crazy."

"I promise, Mama."

"What if Jamal found out? Think about it."

Karma stayed silent, tears running down her face.

Karma's mom shook her head in disapproval. "He would have divorced you and shipped you back to Bilaq. You'll be a divorced woman living with me and your dad. Imagine how miserable you'll be. Divorced, childless, with a crazy mind. No one would marry you."

After she hung up the phone, Karma went outside on her front porch and sipped mint lemonade. She observed her garden with its colorful flowers. The Black-Eyed Susan was the healthiest of all. Veronica was right; it didn't require much work. It blossomed on its own against all the odds.

Veronica's house had been put up for sale a few days after Dom's death.

A week after she spoke with her mom, Karma drove by her house and looked at the "for sale" sign.

Who would buy this house? What crazy family would buy a home where someone killed themselves? Who would want to live in a horror house, a cursed place?

Apparently, someone didn't care. The house was eventually sold less than a month after the incident. Karma marveled as the sign changed from Under Contract to Sold. The house where she spent wonderful evenings and made many memories was sold to a single, middle-aged man who kept to himself and rarely left the house.

What actually happened to Dom? Karma thought repeatedly. She had promised herself that she would find out what had driven him to end his life. She owed it to him. She owed it to Veronica.

Chapter 5

KARMA THOUGHT HER days of forming friendships were over. Then, one day, almost three weeks later, she met Jill in the woods. Jill was tall, skinny—way too skinny, as if she was malnourished—with arms like sticks, hollow cheeks, and significant bags under her eyes. Her face was pale, and she had no makeup on. Karma never left the house without makeup! Not even when she walked Baladi just around the block. Vanity was a Bilaqi woman's middle name.

When Karma met Jill for the first time, she was wearing cropped black yoga pants and a pink sleeveless shirt. Her black hair was tied up in a ponytail. Around her neck was a wireless headphone of some sort. Jill reminded Karma of the actress Demi Moore. She'd grown up watching her movies in Bilaq—A Few Good Men, Ghost, and GI Jane.

Jill was walking a small dog with a missing hind leg. The dog hopped along the trail, unleashed as if nothing were wrong.

Karma, walking Baladi on the opposite side of the trail, stopped and waved. Baladi immediately approached the three-legged dog and sniffed it. The three-legged dog licked him.

"What happened to his leg?" asked Karma.

"It's a she. This is Mia," said Jill, looking at her dog and smiling.

Karma waved at the dog. "Hi, Mia."

"I don't know what happened to her leg. I adopted her like that."

"Oh! Really? Why would you adopt a dog missing a leg?" Karma asked, raising her eyebrows. She immediately wished she hadn't asked that question, wondering if her inquiry was a bit insensitive, especially since Americans tend to be easily offended.

Jill smiled. "Well, I figured if I don't adopt her, no one else would, and they might euthanize her. I felt I needed to do something."

"Oh wow. That's so nice of you," said Karma, suddenly feeling bad about her husband buying a fancy dog instead of adopting a needy one. Why did Jamal spend so much money on a dog when he could have rescued one for a fraction of the price? He had bragged about the cost on several occasions. They could have saved a dog from being euthanized instead. Was it all to impress her?

"Can I pet her?" asked Karma.

Jill nodded. "Yeah, sure. She's very friendly."

Mia sat quietly and let Karma pet her.

"Good girl, Mia," said Karma, inhaling the cold fall breeze. "Does she not have a leash?"

"She doesn't need one. She's always beside me."

Karma kept petting Mia. "Lucky you. That is not the case here. My dog would run all over the neighborhood without a leash on."

"You know... You can train him to walk without a leash, right? Is your dog a lab?" asked Jill.

"We're not sure," Karma lied. "We adopted him from a shelter." It wasn't the best way to start a new friendship, but it couldn't end up worse than her previous one. "We discussed doing a DNA test on him, but we never got around to it." Another lie.

A few days after their first encounter, Karma kept bumping into Jill in the woods. Jill was talkative and seemed eager to make a new friend. Karma trod carefully. She was still not over what had happened with Veronica and even questioned if she deserved any new friends.

She didn't want to ruin another life like she had done with Veronica's.

Karma did everything she could to avoid touching Jill. The last thing she wanted was another destructive vision. She maintained a three-foot perimeter—no hugging, no tugging, no handshaking.

Sometimes, Jill was more talkative than Karma was in the mood for. She told her about her deadbeat of a husband, whom she'd quickly gotten rid of. She told her about her teenage daughter, who was glued to her phone and barely left the house. "She never talks to me! I miss when she was a baby who wanted cuddles."

Jill told Karma about her time in Iraq, where she served with the U.S. Army. Karma swallowed hard, even though Jill didn't look at her with the same prejudice with which so many service people regarded Middle Easterners.

"Our SUV flipped over on one of the dirt roads," she shared. "I destroyed my back. Even the top docs at Walter Reed couldn't fix me. Got an honorable discharge and can never work again because of the injuries."

Karma's hand flew over her mouth. "That's terrible. I'm so sorry."

Jill sighed heavily. 'The pain is paralyzing. Sometimes I stay in bed for days."

Karma felt uncomfortable whenever Jill mentioned her Iraq days. How many Iraqis did she kill? How would her mom feel if she knew she was friends with an American soldier?

Karma had so many questions she didn't dare to ask Jill. Did Jill even remember that Bilaq had stood with Iraq during the war? How did she feel about that? Did she view Karma as the enemy? Why did Jill ever want to hang out with her? All they seemed to have in common was their dogs; even their dogs were so different.

As time went on, something about Jill bothered Karma: her limp, which was sometimes very pronounced and sometimes not present at all. Also, the way she talked. Her speech was slow, which at first Karma had thought was because English wasn't Karma's first language.

But one morning, Karma recognized it as something else: intoxication, perhaps? At ten o'clock in the morning! She looked closely at Jill's face, her red eyes, her constricted pupils.

What's wrong with this woman? Is she sick? Is she on medication?

"Everything okay?" Jill asked. "Do I have something on my face?"

Karma quickly switched her attention to Baladi.

"You have a new friend," Jamal noted when she mentioned Jill casually over dinner. "Do I get to meet this one?"

"Oh, we aren't really friends," she said. Karma didn't want to get closer to Jill.

"That's too bad. I was hoping she would help you get over what happened with Veronica."

"I doubt it," said Karma, gaze fixed on her plate of rice and ground beef.

Meanwhile, Jill insisted on hanging out. "Seriously, you've never been to the city's indoor swimming pool? Let's go! Today! What else do you have to do?"

Grocery shopping and dinner preparation. Karma didn't have a good excuse.

"Swimming helps my back," Jill said. "I just do laps for an hour or so, and I feel completely refreshed."

Karma didn't even know what laps were. She had never learned how to swim and was ashamed to admit that. "Swimming is just not my thing. I'm more of a walker."

How do Americans find the time to engage in all these activities and acquire these skills? They swim, kayak, hike, ride horses, ski, skate, and bike. She never did any of these things. Would she ever be able to fit into this society?

"How did you meet your husband again?" Jill asked her one day as they were walking their dogs together.

Why does she keep asking about Jamal? She suddenly remembered what her mom had told her about American women and keeping them away from her husband.

"He is a catch. Those American women would want to steal him from you." My mom and her silly, backward thinking!

Karma didn't want her to judge, so she gave an answer inspired by one of her romance novels. "Online." Karma felt bad about lying. I've been lying a lot lately. Has this country done this to me?

"Lucky you to meet a doctor online," Jill said. "I never got that lucky. I once matched with a tow truck driver."

"We just connected," Karma said, her voice laced with false cheerfulness.

Jill's face lit up with a big smile. "What's his specialty? Where does he work? Does he have a private practice? I totally want to meet him!"

Karma gave short answers, trying to change the subject subtly. Was Jill trying to steal her husband? Could my mom be right?

Jill got lucky. They walked by her house as Jamal was getting home from work an hour earlier than he usually did.

"Hey! Great to meet Karma and Baladi's new friends," he said, reaching down to pet Mia.

"I was afraid she was trying to keep us apart," Jill said, thrusting her hand into Jamal's. A sick feeling overtook Karma.

"She likes to keep her life compartmentalized," Jamal said.

Karma wasn't even sure what that meant.

"I've been eager to meet you. I'm not sure whether Karma mentioned it, but I've been suffering from back pain for over fifteen years now," Jill told Jamal.

Was she trying to get his sympathy? Was this part of her plan? Karma placed a hand on her belly, wishing she had a baby growing there, something to tether Jamal to her forever.

"That's awful! Sorry to hear that," said Jamal as he leaned against the trunk of his car.

Karma pulled Baladi over to stand next to him, planting a kiss on his cheek.

Jill retrieved a baggie for the poop Mia had left on their lawn. "What kind of pain medication do you recommend?" Jill asked, taking a step forward and getting closer to him.

"Oh, probably Aleve or maybe Advil," Jamal said, standing up suddenly and eager to get inside the house.

"Would you prescribe something stronger for severe cases?" Jill asked, twirling a strand of her black hair.

Is she flirting?

"For my most severe patients," her husband said in an all-business voice, "usually post-op, we talk about a pain regimen, but you know most doctors try to avoid narcotics unless absolutely necessary. I'm more inclined to prescribe medical marijuana instead."

"Yeah, I should try that," said Jill.

A FEW DAYS later, Jill called at eleven o'clock in the evening, begging for pain meds.

"Please? I ran out. And it hurts so much," Jill cried into the phone.

"Who is calling at this hour?" Jamal angrily whispered from their master bathroom. "Whoever it is, I'm not here. If it were the hospital, they'd call my cell."

"Sorry," said Karma, the phone glued to her ear. "What did you say?"

"I ran out. I'm in so much pain," said Jill, her voice strained.

"Oh, no. I'm so sorry to hear it," Karma said. "Did you try Aleve or Advil?"

"I need something stronger. Does your husband keep anything on hand?"

Jamal emerged from the bathroom in his boxers, looking annoyed. He would flip if she told him she had to go to Jill's house for her medications.

"No, I'm sorry. He's not here, so I can't ask him," she lied.

The next morning, Karma felt terrible about lying to Jill. The poor woman was in pain, so she stopped by CVS, grabbed two bottles of ibuprofen, and put them in her dog-walking bag.

In the woods, she ran into Jill, strolling while her dog trotted next to her, unleashed. It was an unusually hot day for early fall.

Karma was so relieved to see she was well enough to take a walk, even a slow one. "How are you feeling today? Better, I hope! Just in case you're not, here you go." Karma handed her the bottles.

Jill looked at the bottle, her dark circles under her eyes visible. "What's this for?" Jill asked, tilting her head. Beads of sweat dotted her forehead.

Maybe she was feeling better than she looked. "Remember last night? You called me. You said you ran out of meds."

Jill's shoulders sagged. "Oh. Last night. Right." Jill fell quiet, then looked up and focused on a biker who passed by, saying, "On your left!"

Wait. Did Jill even remember she had called the night before? "Do you still need it?" asked Karma. What's up with this woman? Really?

Jill's eyes darted away momentarily, then back to Karma. "Oh, yeah, of course. The pain is excruciating. Thank you again. Let's hang out soon."

Karma had always wondered what Jill did for a living, but she never dared ask. One day, Jill opened up about her "hustle." She spent a significant portion of her time refurbishing furniture.

"I found my calling later in life," she told her as they both stood in the front yard of Karma's house.

Karma raised an eyebrow. "What exactly do you do?"

"I get old furniture, restore it, then resell it for a profit."

Karma nodded slowly, absorbing this new information. "Oh. I see. Where do you get the furniture from?"

She shrugged. "Ah, everywhere—online, estate sales, rich people's curbsides, trash," she laughed.

"Really? You just pick that stuff up?" asked Karma as she petted Baladi, who was eyeing Jill's dog.

Jill tucked a strand of her silky black hair behind her ear. "Oh yeah. You have no idea what people throw away: chairs, tables, desks. All are in excellent condition. My friends think I'm crazy for doing this, given my terrible back issues. But you know, I'm willing to tolerate the pain of doing something I love."

"You must really enjoy it to be willing to withstand all that pain," said Karma.

She smiled. "I love it. You know what? I can take you with me one day when I go hunting."

"Hunting?"

"Yeah, I'm looking for furniture. You'd love it. It's quite the adventure," said Jill with a twinkle in her eyes.

She really must love what she does.

❋ ❋ ❋

As promised, Jill picked up Karma in her worn-out Ford truck one morning. When she got in, Karma couldn't help but notice the disarray inside the vehicle: McDonald's coffee cups on the floor, plastic bags scattered everywhere, paint cans on the back seat, and even a half-eaten burger inside the cup holder.

"Sorry about the mess," said Jill.

"Don't worry about it. You should see my car," she lied. She didn't even drive; she was too afraid of the highways to venture outside on her own, instead letting Jamal do all the driving and keeping their Honda SUV in pristine shape, insisting that no eating or drinking was allowed inside the car.

When did lying become so easy?

They stopped by an estate sale, then visited a yard sale, and finally drove through an affluent neighborhood, where they saw big mansions with large yards and elaborate landscaping, as well as Mercedes and BMWs in the driveways.

"You know, I picked this day because it's the day before big trash day. That's when they leave the good stuff outside. The day before."

Karma could not help but be impressed by Jill's determination and her industrious nature. She really went after what she wanted, whatever it took, to make it happen.

Karma offered to help Jill haul the furniture into the back of the truck: two wooden chairs, a desk, and a table.

As Karma was carrying one of the wicker chairs, she felt a sharp pain in her back. "AH!" she shouted.

"Are you okay?" asked Jill.

Karma froze in place, scared to move. "I pulled something in my back."

"Carefully, put the chair down. Can you walk?" Jill asked, touching Karma's arm. "I'll take care of the rest. Next time, we'll hire movers. We can't afford to have both of us with busted backs!"

Karma wasn't listening; an image was forming. Jill had touched her. She tried to suppress it, but the pain was excruciating, and it hampered her ability to obstruct the clear-as-day vision.

Jill was in the woods at dusk, talking to a teenager with pitch-black hair that reached the middle of her back. Not just any teenager, but one with red Converse shoes. Dom's girlfriend, Danielle. Danielle handed her something, a small object. Jill handed something back. A wad of cash. Jill exchanged a few words with Danielle. Danielle's face morphed in anger. She opened her mouth and screamed, then lunged at Jill, grabbing her arm with both hands.

Jill pulled back, but Danielle held tight, so tight, with what seemed like a force that would break stones. Crack! Jill screamed as she looked at her arm, snapped in half, the shape of a bone protruding under the skin. Jill kept screaming and then fell to the ground.

Karma shook her head as the vision disappeared.

"Are you okay?" asked Jill. "You look as though you've seen a ghost."

"I might have seen one." Karma clenched her jaw. *Shit! Did I just say that? Did I just slip like this?*

Jill laughed.

"I'm joking. I'm just in a lot of pain," Karma said.

Jill had opened the car door for her and moved like she was going to help Karma into the truck, but Karma didn't want to see more. She gritted her teeth and climbed into the cab on her own, swallowing the pain.

"Ice it, and you'll be okay. That handsome husband of yours will take good care of you. After all, he is a doctor." Jill closed the door.

They drove back home in silence.

Karma couldn't find the words. Why would Danielle do that to Jill? What had they been exchanging? Why was this happening again with someone she had just befriended?

It's going to be like Veronica all over again.

Karma again found herself plagued by a vision she didn't understand. Whereas her visions when she was younger were straightforward—a person got injured, fell in love, or moved away—with first Dom and now Jill, she felt not only too close to the subjects but also hopeless to help them avoid the fate she saw.

What was Jill doing in the woods with those teenagers? What was she doing with Danielle, Dom's girlfriend? And why would Danielle do this horrible thing to her? Was this vision even real or a fluke response to pain? She knew the answer; her visions were always real.

THE NEXT DAY, Karma walked Baladi in silence through a trail in the woods, the only sound made by leaves crackling under her feet. Baladi stopped to sniff a white poodle on the trail. She waved at the dog owner, a petite blonde woman whom she hadn't seen before, then shifted her attention to her dog as he sniffed the poodle's behind.

"Cute dog," said the woman. "A lab?"

"Yeah. Pure," she said, expecting to feel proud. She didn't. Instead, she felt guilty.

As she was heading home, she passed by a bus stop at the corner of the street. A huge ad covered the side of the bus stop shelter. She might have seen that ad at least 100 times before. But this time, she stopped and looked, really looked.

The ad showed a shadow of a man trapped inside an orange transparent medicine bottle. The man had his arms extended, with his hands touching the edge of the bottle as if he were trying to break free. The ad bore the following message: "Painkillers are easy to get into. Hard to escape."

Suddenly, something clicked.

Jill. Her back pain. The painkillers she wanted. Her interest in Jamal's work. Everything suddenly fell into place. Jill was addicted to drugs, like this man in the ad.

In the vision, was she buying drugs from Danielle? Was it a drug deal gone wrong, which happened all the time on the crime shows she watched? Was Danielle a dealer? Dom too? Was that why he killed himself?

Karma's skin tingled, and her knees began to shake.

She had to do something. She could redeem herself.

When she got home, she knew she should make dinner and move a load of laundry over before Jamal got home. Instead, she went online. Karma read for hours about opioids, about what was happening in the country she now called home. She learned about addiction, the pharmaceutical companies' role, and the FDA's regulations.

She forgot about dinner.

She called Jamal and told him she wasn't feeling well, asking him to pick up some Chinese food on her way home. However, she failed to move the laundry to the dryer.

"Do you deal with opioid patients?" she asked Jamal during dinner as she chewed on a steamed dumpling. Opioids. That was the first time she said that word out loud.

"Yeah, we see them in the ER all the time. Why do you ask?" he said, tilting his head.

"Just curious. I saw a documentary about drug addiction in the US on TV, and I'm a bit shocked. Had no idea it was that common here." She hated herself for lying to him, but what choice did she have? If she told him she suspected Jill, he might not let her be friends with her anymore.

"Yeah. It's a huge problem fueled by irresponsible doctors and greedy pharmaceutical companies," he said, grabbing some noodles with his chopsticks.

"Does it mainly affect the poor?" she asked, twirling her fork. She'd never learned how to use chopsticks.

He shook his head. "Oh no, you'd be surprised. It affects the rich and the educated. It's a huge problem. Terrible addiction. I lost a number of my patients to opioids."

"They overdose?"

"Yep. Usually, they are on something harder than the pharmaceutical they originally got hooked on. They turn to heroin when they can't get their scripts refilled or find pills on the street."

Karma took in a large gulp of air. "Is it common among women?"

Jamal snagged a piece of eggroll. "Yeah. I'd say it's equal between men and women."

She fidgeted in her chair. "Thank you for picking up dinner. I'll walk the dog, and then when I return, I'll clean up."

"Are you okay?" he said, taking a sip from his water cup. "You seem sad or preoccupied by something."

"Just tired," she smiled nervously. "You know, fertility hormones and all of that." Oh shit! When was the last time I took the hormones? Shit, shit, shit!

"Yeah, those! They can really mess with you. I can walk the dog if you want?" he offered, then held her hand across the dining table.

She squeezed his hand. "Thanks, babes. I need some fresh air. I'll be back soon."

He glanced out the window. "It's getting dark. Please stay safe."

"Don't worry, Habibi. I have Baladi by my side. He'll protect me from all the monsters and the ghosts," she said, smiling.

She looked at him and realized that she was in love with this handsome, caring man. No, he wasn't perfect. He could get angry sometimes, but who was perfect? Certainly not her, with her visions, her tendency to lie, and now her forgetfulness about taking the hormones that were intended to give her her heart's desire. As her mom had told her, she was even lucky to have found love in the first place, given her condition.

Outside, Karma sniffed the crisp October air and tugged Baladi by her side. She reminded herself of her mom's advice: Never get involved in people's affairs. Look what had happened to Dom and Veronica.

She walked down her street and decided to do the street tour instead of the woods tour. She ran into familiar dog walkers—the white woman with a Border Collie, the Asian man with two Chihuahuas, the husky white man with a German Shepherd, the young interracial couple with a pregnant woman, and a toddler with a white Lab. She loved the melting pot, the idea of America that you would be welcomed no matter where you came from, that you would make it as long as you worked hard.

She waved, said hellos, and let Baladi sniff all the dogs.

As she contemplated her recent vision, she stopped on the sidewalk, took out her phone, and looked up. "How many people die from opioids daily?" She got the following answer: "2018 data shows that every day, 128 people in the United States die after overdosing on opioids."

128! Jill could easily be one of those.

She had to rescue her. Karma couldn't let her be a statistic. She kept on reading as she walked Baladi. She almost bumped into a tree trunk, but she didn't care. She learned about the most common types of opioids, names she had never heard of before: Vicodin, oxycodone, morphine, codeine, fentanyl.

WHEN SHE COULDN'T sleep that night, she FaceTimed with her mom.

"Why are you still up?" her mom asked. "What time is it there?"

Glancing at the clock with heavy eyes, Karma replied in a weary voice, "Three AM."

"What's on your mind?"

Karma told her about Jill.

Her mom leaned closer to the camera, emphasizing her words, "Karma, don't ever get involved in this. Let the Americans sort it out among themselves. Drugs and all of that. This is dangerous stuff. Stay away."

"But haram, Jill. I feel bad for her." Karma felt guilty for even thinking for a second that Jill was after Jamal when, clearly, she was after a refill.

"You can't fix people's problems." She could hear her mom's voice getting louder. "Stay away. This is some dangerous territory you are getting yourself into. And stop touching people."

Yes, she needed to put a force field around her and be more mindful of her personal space. "Okay, how is Baba?" Karma asked, trying to shift the topic.

"He's fine. He's making me coffee."

A whiff of her dad's famous Turkish coffee made her feel nostalgic. She missed her dad, her sweet father, who had made coffee for her mom and brought it to bed every morning throughout their thirty-year marriage.

She wanted to be back in the comfort and safety of her own home, where she could be with her people—those who looked like her, spoke like her, and behaved like her.

Right before she finally closed her eyes, she had an epiphany: Her mom was wrong. She was given this gift for a reason. She was meant to save people.

She woke up determined to confront Danielle.

First Dom, now Jill. Clearly, she was the source. Jill was just a victim, just like Dom had been.

Chapter 6

THE NEXT MORNING, Jamal left early for work. He told her he had major surgery and had had a hard time sleeping the night before. Karma had struggled to give him her full attention as he tossed and turned and woke up several times during the night.

"Don't worry about breakfast," said Jamal as he left the house with a mug of hot coffee in hand. "I'll grab some on the way."

As Karma munched on her zaatar toast and a cup of hot Lipton tea, she mapped out her day.

She had to finish all her chores before the high school kids would be let out. She knew their schedule from the many times she walked by the high school with Baladi and marveled at how different their high school experience was from hers. She had gone to an all-girls high school in Bilaq, and boys had always been an enigma. In her newly adopted country, things were completely the opposite. Girls mixed with boys and openly displayed their attraction freely and without restraint. Boys' arms around girls, boys hugging girls, and boys kissing girls. Unlike her school, no one wore uniforms. Instead, everyone looked as if they were going to the mall—jeans, T-shirts, sneakers, AirPods, and even pajamas. How could they be serious about school when they were dressed like that? As for kids driving themselves to school, that was something else. First, where did they get these cars from? Did their parents buy them cars? At sixteen? She didn't even own a bike at sixteen.

Danielle should be there when school is over. Where else would she be?

At precisely five minutes past the three o'clock bell, Danielle emerged from the main school gate as Karma waited by the sidewalk across the street with Baladi, who was busy observing all the kids, his tail wagging in excitement. Karma stood beside a tree, hoping its tall branches would make a good hide-away. Danielle was not alone; she was with a tall boy who had his arm around her. The boy was nothing like Dom. He had short black hair and earrings in his ears and nose. They were both dressed in black jeans and white shirts as if they had matched their outfits. Danielle's long black hair looked disheveled as if she had awakened from a nap.

How do their parents let them leave the house looking like that?

The boy must have made a joke because Danielle laughed. Then they kissed right in front of everyone, including the other kids, the teachers, and the bus drivers. Karma's cheeks flushed.

She waited, pretending to adjust Baladi's harness while spying on Danielle and her new boyfriend from around the corner.

The memory of Veronica's fears washed over her. Danielle was bad news; it seemed that her mere presence hurt those around her. She had to stop Danielle from hurting Jill, the only friend she had left in this town.

Danielle and her boyfriend started walking, his arm still slung over her shoulders.

Karma crossed the street and trailed behind them, keeping at least six feet away. They walked for ten minutes, oblivious to the world around them. They laughed, kissed, and held hands, lost in their own world.

How did she forget about Dom so quickly? How long has it been—a month? Two months? She is heartless, that crazy teenager.

Karma followed them, hoping Baladi wouldn't stop to do his business and make her lose sight of them.

Baladi kept on padding, stopping briefly to sniff a couple of bushes. They stopped by her single-story house with pastel yellow siding and walked to the front door, where they both removed their shoes, leaving them on the front porch.

Curious. Were those Danielle's house rules? No shoes inside?

Right before they went in, Danielle turned her head and looked at Karma.

Karma's heart dropped. Was she caught?

Even from a distance, Karma could make out how Danielle's face changed. Her eyes bulged, and her face turned red. She let out a loud cry, some sort of howl that Karma couldn't decipher.

Like in the vision, except directed at her. In real life. Karma took a deep breath. It's all in my head. I'm imagining this. Danielle then turned her head and went inside the house along with her boyfriend. Karma clenched her shaking hands and then let out a deep breath. She walked Baladi up and down the street a couple of times, waiting for them to re-emerge. Still, there was no sign of Danielle or her boyfriend. Karma's feet started to ache, and it was time to feed Baladi.

She'd started to head home when a blue Toyota Corolla passed by the house and stopped in the driveway. A middle-aged woman—an older version of Danielle—got out of the car. She had the same dark, long hair, fair complexion, and pointed nose. The woman was wearing pink scrubs. Was she a nurse? Was that where Danielle was getting her drugs from? Was her mom in on it?

Karma's head throbbed. It was time to head home. She couldn't keep waiting.

When she got home, her phone beeped—a text message from Jamal. "How are things? The surgery went well. I'll be home in a few hours."

Karma sighed. She was not in the mood for her husband or his needs. She kicked back on the sofa, closed her eyes, and replayed the events of the day. She contemplated taking a nap, calling her mom, or maybe scrolling through her Instagram feed, but the pull of Danielle drew her back outside for another walk.

With Baladi on a leash, she left the house for Danielle's place. She was already exhausted from all the walking back and forth that day. When she got there, she noticed their shoes were still outside the front door.

What are they doing inside? How many babies have they made already?

Karma went up and down the street across from Danielle's house several times, then decided she was going home. Her legs were shaking, and she felt she was already drawing attention. Also, Jamal would be home soon, and she would have a lot of explaining to do. As she started walking home, she heard some commotion, and then, from the corner of her eye, she saw Danielle and her boyfriend emerge from the house. Danielle was smiling, a backpack hanging from her shoulder. They put on their shoes and left the house. Daniel adjusted her bag, then held her boyfriend's hand.

Karma clenched her jaw and prayed for Baladi to stay quiet.

She waited thirty seconds, crossed the street, and started walking behind them, making sure to leave enough distance between them. They were oblivious to their surroundings. He had his arm around her, and occasionally, they would stop briefly and kiss.

All that kissing! Where are they headed?

They took a turn and then started walking down the street.

The woods!

Karma and Baladi trailed behind them.

Suddenly, Karma knew what was about to go down. She had seen that same scene.

She followed them as they moved silently along the paved trail in the woods, then turned left toward a more wooded, unpaved area.

Clearly, Jill would be there.

Her vision had been accurate.

She had to stop Danielle from giving Jill drugs and from breaking Jill's arm. The poor woman already had a bad back. How would she do her furniture restoration with two severe injuries?

Karma couldn't stop thinking about the weird howl that Danielle had let out. She wondered if it was the result of the drugs, if they could mess with someone's head so much that they became inhuman, unrelatable.

Baladi stopped at least twice during their walk to relieve himself, slowing them down. Karma increased her pace until she caught up with Danielle and her boyfriend.

The path was uneven, dotted with exposed roots and fallen branches. Towering oak and maple trees formed a lush canopy overhead, their leaves whispering in the gentle breeze.

"Hey, hey, Danielle, stop!" shouted Karma as she was running to catch up with them.

Both Danielle and her boyfriend turned around.

"I know what you're doing," said Karma, still catching her breath.

Danielle tilted her head as a frown began to form on her face.

The smell of rosewater made Karma dizzy. She suddenly felt nostalgic, then disoriented, as if she had lost touch with reality.

She was transferred back to Bilaq when she was ten. Sitting in a chair in her mother's kitchen, she watched her mother make rice pudding with rosewater.

"Remember what I told you about those visions of yours," Karma's mother said as she poured two spoons of rosewater into the pudding mix. "Don't let them control you."

"I can't stop them," Karma said, tears welling in her eyes. "They're always there. They never leave me."

"Of course you can!" her mom said. "I already explained what to do. Think happy thoughts. Think of when we went to the beach last summer."

Karma shook her head slightly, getting her mind out of that memory. She was back in the woods with that witch. She looked at Danielle. "You sell drugs. Narcotics. I know! I saw you! Leave my friend Jill alone. Don't hurt her."

Danielle's eyes were bloodshot. She kept staring at Karma. Her cheeks suddenly reddened, and then she let out a terrifying, inhuman howl, rattling the trees in the woods. Karma's heart dropped. Goosebumps crawled all over her skin.

Who was she? What was she?

Upon hearing the howl, Baladi barked and growled, crouching in a charging position, ready to attack Danielle. Karma quickly tightened her grip on his leash to stop him from advancing.

Danielle stared silently at Karma, and then, without warning, she charged. Before Karma could react, Danielle's long, black, manicured nails gouged the right side of her face, right behind her eye. Karma cried out in agony. She let go of Baladi and put her hands on her face to wipe the dripping blood. Baladi barked and leaped at Danielle, and she slammed her booted foot into his head.

"Don't touch my dog, you crazy bitch," said Karma as she shifted her attention to a whimpering Baladi. Karma was surprised to hear herself say the word "bitch" out loud.

Throughout this, Danielle's boyfriend stood there, watching the scene unfold. He didn't seem fazed by what was happening, as if he had seen her behave this way before. He quietly held Danielle's hand and pulled her closer to him. "Come on, let's get out of here," he said, his voice hoarse.

Karma watched them go, clinging to Baladi's leash, her wounds stinging her face. She pulled some tissues from her bag and dabbed at her cheek. The bleeding hadn't stopped yet.

Danielle could still hurt Jill. She must stop this monster.

As she walked away, Danielle turned her head, looked at Karma with her bloody eyes, and let out another howl, which reverberated in the woods.

Dizzy, Karma fell to the ground. She didn't know how much time had passed, but when she opened her eyes, a middle-aged woman with gray hair was looking down at her.

Looking down with a sense of urgency in her voice, the woman asked, "Are you okay? Can you hear me? Do you need help?"

Baladi was barking beside her. The woman extended her hand and helped her to her feet.

"I must have passed out. I'm okay," said Karma.

"Do you want me to call an ambulance?" the woman asked, her eyes scanning Karma for injuries.

"I'm okay, thank you. I think I'm dehydrated," Karma said while trying to maintain her balance.

"I don't think it's a good idea for you to walk home alone," the woman said, snatching her cell phone from her fleece jacket and offering it to Karma.

"I'm fine," Karma snapped.

"Okay, if you say so," said the woman, giving Karma one last concerned look before continuing along the pathway.

Karma dragged herself back home, Baladi walking beside her. While her heart pounded in fear and her face was seared from the scratches, all she could think of was her failure.

She'd failed Jill just as she'd failed Veronica. The same story, the same plot. Why did she even bother to solve people's issues when a higher power had already sealed their fate? She wondered.

I can never go against what a higher power wants. I will just get hurt.

Once again, my mother is right.

Chapter 7

THE FIRST THING Karma noticed when she got home was Jamal's car in the driveway.

Shit, shit. What would she tell him? That a crazy drug dealer attacked her? He'd never let her walk in the woods again.

Maybe I shouldn't walk in the woods again.

"Hi, babe, is that you?" Jamal asked from the kitchen, where he was drinking a glass of water. "I was just about to call you. It's late, and I was worried about you. Is everything okay?" He put down the glass of water on the counter and looked at her intensely. She could see fine lines under his eyes. Are these new? Am I aging him?

"Sorry, Habibi. I had some drama," she said, facing him across the kitchen counter.

"Oh, my God! What happened to your face?" he asked as soon as he noticed the scratches on her face.

"Don't worry, babe. Just scratched from a neighbor's dog who got too excited. You know how puppies are!" She leaned against the kitchen counter. Baladi brushed against her leg, and she petted him.

"Come here. Let me see you," he said, extending his arm toward her.

She walked toward him. Jamal held her face in his hands, and she could smell the sweat on him. She took a step back.

"Come closer," he commanded. She obliged.

"Oh my!" he said, his eyebrows raised. "That dog really did a number on you. What's wrong with its owner? How do they allow this?" He sighed. "Let's clean this up first." Karma wondered if Jamal, as a doctor, could really tell that it was not just a scratch and that she was lying, but he was too nice to admit his doubts.

Karma removed Baladi's harness and leash, placing him in the crate near the kitchen.

Jamal grabbed her hand and led her to the upstairs bathroom, where the first aid kit was located. "What happened exactly?" he asked while rummaging through the medicine cabinet.

"It's not a big deal. I ran across a neighbor who had a small dog. I kneeled to pet him, and he got too excited and jumped up, scratching my face. It wasn't malicious; it was just excitement."

"Seriously? What kind of dog was it?" Jamal asked while applying Neosporin cream to his face.

"I don't know. A mixed breed, maybe. You know, not pure like ours," she said. "His name is Chicken Nugget." Oh, my God! Chicken Nugget! Couldn't I come up with a better name?

"Ha! What an unusual name," said Jamal.

"I thought so." Karma suddenly felt aroused. Jamal tending to her made her want him. She ached for him to be inside of her at that moment. She knew better, though. She was scratched, damaged goods, and he wouldn't touch her until she healed. She felt hurt and rejected.

"Weird. It looks more like a cat scratch to me," he said, taking a closer look at her face.

"I told you. It was a small dog!" she said, afraid she had already been exposed. "Will it leave a scar?"

He squinted his eyes, taking a closer look at the wound. "I don't think so."

✹ ✹ ✹

RIGHT BEFORE GOING to bed, Karma texted Jill.

Karma: Hey. I'm just checking to see if you want to meet tomorrow. Maybe we can go for another hunt?

Five minutes passed before she got a response.

Jill: You won't believe what happened today. I fell down the stairs and broke my arm.

A white lie. She'd forgive her.

Karma: Oh my goodness, I'm so sorry to hear that. Are you okay? Did you go to the hospital? Please let me know if you need any help.

Jill: I've already been to the doctor for an X-ray and other tests. My arm is broken and in a cast. It should heal in a few weeks.

Karma: So sorry. I'm here if you need anything.

That night, Karma had a hard time sleeping. She couldn't purge the image of Danielle lunging at her from her mind. And that howl! That monstrous howl. The thought sent shivers up and down her spine. And those eyes. Those bloody demonic eyes!

And after all that, she'd hurt Jill.

She had to stop Danielle from hurting Jill even more.

The next morning, as soon as Jamal left for work, Karma called the vet, saying a homeless man had attacked her dog, but so far, he seemed fine. She was worried about what kind of damage that bitch Danielle had done to Baladi. The vet advised her to keep an eye on the dog and bring him to the clinic if he was not acting himself in a few days. She left Baladi in his crate and started walking toward Danielle's house. She needed to focus; she couldn't be distracted by the dog.

It was a crisp fall morning, and the walk to Danielle's house was pleasant. Karma said hi to a few neighbors who asked about Baladi.

"He's still asleep," she responded. "He had a busy day yesterday. We took him to the dog park for the first time!" Another lie.

When she got to Danielle's house, it was 9:30 a.m. Danielle should have already been at school. Karma noticed the Toyota Corolla was still parked in the driveway. Her mom should be home.

She walked to the front porch and rang the bell. She looked at the bare spot under the floor-to-ceiling front window, noticing that it was nothing but dirt. Why didn't they plant anything there? A few perennials would look great in that spot. She suddenly thought of Veronica and realized how much she missed her.

Danielle's mom partially opened the door and peeked her head through the opening. She was already dressed in her pink scrubs, with her name tag reading "Kathy."

"Hi, Kathy," said Karma.

"No, thank you," she responded. "Whatever you're selling, I'm not buying." Kathy slammed the door.

Karma was taken aback by the rejection. She let out a big sigh and rang the bell again.

"Please go away," said Kathy, peeking her head through the door.

Karma smiled. "I'm Karma. Your neighbor."

Karma noticed Kathy's eyes were red and watery as if she had been crying.

"I don't care who you are. Please go away," said Kathy, then let out a small cry that started to get louder. She covered her hands with her face and started wailing.

"Are you okay? Do you need help?" asked Karma.

"Please leave me alone."

Karma left the house and walked back home, shoulders slumped, head down.

What had she been thinking? Why would Danielle's mother ever talk to a complete stranger?

THE NEXT DAY, at the same time, she showed up at Kathy's house with flowers from her garden: daffodils, sunflowers, and pansies.

"You again!" said Kathy as soon as she opened the door, dressed in bright pink scrubs.

"I just wanted to check on you. Hope these flowers will cheer you up," Karma said, handing her the flowers.

Kathy looked surprised. "Thank you. They're beautiful."

"They're from my garden."

"How nice. Gardening is not my thing," said Kathy, leaning against the door frame. Karma contemplated brushing her fingers against Kathy; maybe she would see something, something that would reveal all this drama with Danielle, but she decided against it. What would Kathy's reaction be if she touched her?

Ah, Americans and their personal space! So hard to get near them sometimes.

"I can help you," said Karma, pointing at the bare area under the front windows. "We can start with your front porch if you like."

Kathy smiled. "Sorry about the other day. I was very upset. Please come in," she said, motioning for her to come inside.

Karma took one step. "Are you sure? I don't want to impose on you."

"Yeah, please come in. I love meeting new neighbors."

As soon as Karma walked in, she was greeted by the strong smell of cat urine. She knew this scent well, thanks to her mom's cat, which had done its business all over their apartment. She was expecting the house to smell of rosewater, but that was not the case.

Karma looked around the room and was struck by what she saw—empty pizza boxes on the sofa in the middle of the main room, a cat bowl placed on a stained white carpet, books, plastic bags, and shoes scattered on the floor. There was mail, empty Amazon boxes, and dirty dishes on the small dining table at the end of the room. There was a bra hanging on a dining chair.

Her mother would die if she saw this place.

"Sorry about the mess. I've been busy with work. Have a seat," Kathy apologized, removing the pizza boxes from the sofa and placing them on the floor so they could sit comfortably.

"Don't worry about it. I'm not staying long. I need to go back and check on my dog," responded Karma as she sat on the sofa.

"Where do you live?" Kathy asked, sitting on the edge of the sofa, ready to spring up at any moment.

"A few blocks away. On Jasmine Drive."

"Ah, I love that street. It's very quiet. I used to walk there with my daughter when she was young. Ah, well, when she was sweet and used to listen to me. Not anymore, unfortunately," Kathy reflected, her legs moving up and down.

Pausing for a moment as she gathered her thoughts, she said, "I'm actually here with a concern about Danielle."

"You know her? What did she do this time?" she asked, rolling her eyes.

Karma paused, gazing at the floor-to-ceiling windows of the quiet suburban street lined with similar tri-level houses. "Well... um... I saw your daughter sell drugs to one of the neighbors."

Kathy threw her head back. "Drugs? Are you for real?"

Karma bit her lower lip. "Yeah. Narcotics. She actually attacked me when I confronted her."

"What?" exclaimed Kathy, noticing the scratches on Karma's face. "Danielle attacked you? Is that from her?" She touched the marks on Karma's face.

Oh, she touched me, please, please, I need a vision, something.

Nothing came up.

Karma cleared her throat. "Yeah, that's from her."

Kathy shook her head. "That girl! I don't know what to tell you, but my daughter has been having issues."

Karma's eyes widened slightly. "Oh. What kind of issues?"

"Mental health issues," said Kathy, biting her lip. "I don't know why I'm telling you this, but this all started maybe a year ago. She was the sweetest girl. Always had been an A+ student."

Karma glanced at Kathy's clenched fists.

"She was popular. Lots of friends," said Kathy. "She loved sports and crafts. Helped me around the house. Took care of the neighbors' kids, and then one day, she just flipped as if a switch had been turned on. She just became, I don't know how to say it, a witch!"

"A witch?" asked Karma, tilting her head.

Kathy got quiet, and Karma could see tears welling in her eyes. "I took her to a child psychiatrist who threw words like hallucinations and schizophrenia. We still need to do more tests to confirm the diagnosis. He prescribed medication, but she refuses to take it."

Karma suddenly felt guilty for snitching on her. This teenager is sick in the head; she's mentally ill. Majnouneh—crazy. No wonder. "I'm sorry to hear that. Is there anything I can do to help? I'm home and have some time. Let me help you."

Kathy touched Karma's hand. "Honey, I doubt you can. Not even the experts can help her. My daughter thinks... I don't know how to explain it.

She thinks she's possessed by the Devil. Whenever I ask her why she did what she did, she says, 'The Devil made me do it!'"

"The Devil?"

"Yeah, can you believe it? She even has a name for the Devil!"

"A name for the Devil?"

She leaned in closer. "Yeah. In her twisted mind, the Devil is a woman. She calls her Lilith! Lilith made me do this; Lilith made me do that. It's crazy."

Karma raised her eyebrows. "That is crazy!"

"Yeah. I told you she's not well!"

It still didn't excuse her being responsible for Jill's injury and maybe even Dom's death. "I'm so sorry. Please tell me if there is anything I can do." Karma wondered when the last time Kathy had cleaned the litter box.

Kathy looked exhausted. "Nothing, honey. There's nothing you or I can do. Thank you for telling me about the drugs. I don't know where she's getting them from. I'll have to deal with it, but I don't know how." Kathy sighed, closed her eyes, and then opened them again. "She won't listen to me. What shall I do? Call the police? On my own daughter." Tears seeped out of her eyes.

Karma touched Kathy's hand. "I'm sorry it has been so hard."

Still no vision, goddammit!

She rose, ready to leave the house, and noticed an empty dog crate next to a worn-out, black leather sofa in the living room. "Do you have a dog?" Karma asked, pointing at the dog crate in the corner.

"Oh, Scout," said Kathy, then got silent for a bit. "He's no longer with us, unfortunately."

"Oh, I'm so sorry."

"He disappeared."

Karma tilted her head slightly. "What? Disappeared? What happened?"

Kathy let out a long sigh. "When Danielle started having her issues, he got scared of her. And he wouldn't stop barking around her."

"Oh, really?" asked Karma, raising her eyebrows. No wonder Baladi lost his mind when he saw her.

"Yeah, we had had him for ten years, but all of a sudden, he didn't recognize Danielle as if she were a total stranger, and my daughter became mean to him and hit him on the head with a stick a number of times."

Karma's stomach churned. "Oh, geez. That's horrible."

"One day, I returned home, and he was no longer there. He just vanished. Puff!" She threw her hands in the air. "I quizzed Danielle, and she said she was out with her friends all day and had no clue where that 'stinky bastard' was," she said, making air quotes with her fingers. "We never saw him again. I contacted all the animal shelters in the area, asked the neighbors, and posted notes everywhere. Nothing."

Karma felt shivers climbing up her spine. I must protect Baladi from her. "Oh, that's awful. Do you think Danielle had something to do with it?"

She shrugged. "Who knows? I really don't know who she has become. Now, I'm sorry to be rude, but I really must go to work."

Karma left the house and looked out at the quiet suburban street, then turned left to head back home. Her heart dropped. Right in front of her on the porch, less than three feet away, was Danielle, looking straight at her.

What the hell is this dog killer doing here? Isn't she supposed to be in school?

Danielle's eyes were bloodshot, even her irises were red, and her fair skin was even fairer, completely white. She looked like a ghost.

She took a step closer and smirked, showing the whitest teeth Karma had ever seen. Karma could smell rosewater. She felt dizzy and started hyperventilating. She couldn't handle the smell any longer.

An image flashed before her. Karma closed her eyes.

Karma was fourteen. She was in a store in Bilaq, getting some bread. A man stood behind her. He was so close she could hear his heavy breathing.

She quickly paid and left the store. He followed her. She walked faster. He caught up with her and grabbed her arm. He pressed so hard she felt her bones crushing. She knew who he was—the man down the street used to beat his wife until she took the kids and left him. She was so scared she thought her heart would stop; it couldn't take the shock of fear pumping through her veins.

"I know about your little tricks, you dirty bitch," he told her. "You told my wife that I would end up in jail. That's why she left me. She said you could see the future. That I'm a lost cause and that she should leave me."

Karma swallowed. He was right; she had warned his wife about him after seeing her with her clothes ripped, crying by the sidewalk. She had told her about the vision she had had a year before when she'd bumped into the woman's husband at the store. Karma wanted her to leave him. She wanted her to protect herself. She should have listened to her mom, kept to herself, and not let her mind control her. She should not have meddled with the neighbors' affairs. Too late now. He is going to kill me. If only I had listened to my mom.

"Guess what? My wife came back. Your tricks didn't work. If you come near my family again, I will break your bones and throw you to the dogs."

He placed his hand on her shoulder and shoved her. She stumbled but regained her balance. An image formed before her: He was in the hospital, surrounded by doctors. "Sorry," said one of the doctors to his distraught wife. "We tried to save him. It was a massive heart attack."

"Justice will be served," Karma said out loud.

When she opened her eyes, Danielle was still there, staring at her. She was tapping her right foot on the sidewalk, her red Converse shoe marking the rhythm.

Danielle was going to kill her. This crazy teenager was going to kill her and spill her blood in the street. She was the reason Karma was having flashbacks. It was the smell of that damn rosewater. She was hypnotizing her with it.

"You stupid woman," said Danielle, taking a step closer. "You think you can change fate? How dumb you are. Do you think you're some sort of superhero or vigilante?"

Karma felt paralyzed. She tried to open her mouth, but no words came out. She tried to run but couldn't move.

Danielle's voice sounded so mature, the sound of a middle-aged woman, not a dumb teenager. "You think you could have prevented Dom from killing himself? Do you think you can stop Jill from drugging herself up? "

"What are you talking about?" Karma asked. She was starting to feel a splitting headache.

"You know what I'm talking about. You, of all people, should know that your fate is sealed. El makoutb ala el jebeen bitshoufhou el ein. The eye will see what's written on the forehead."

Karma froze. "I didn't know you spoke Arabic."

Danielle smirked. "I didn't know either."

"You're sick in the head. What do you want from me?" she demanded, feeling the ground spin beneath her. She stumbled, then quickly regained her balance.

"Listen, honey, let me tell you something, woman to woman." She smiled. "You really can't mess with fate, so give up this fight. Go home and play with your dog. Fuck your husband and leave things as they were supposed to be. Also, you should try being on top for a change!"

Danielle took a step closer, her face almost touching Karma's.

Karma shivered.

"And that baby of yours? Ha! You're in for a surprise!"

What baby?

Karma didn't remember how she got home. She might have run all the way. Everything in her was shaking: her eyes, her legs, her hands, her arms. When she got home, she rushed to the bathroom and threw up in the toilet.

She washed her face and looked at herself in the mirror. Her face was yellow.

Jamal couldn't see her like this. He could come home any minute. Who knows with his schedule?

She went to the bedroom, applied concealer under her eyes to hide her dark circles, and dabbed on red blush to her cheeks.

She went to the kitchen and grabbed a glass of water. Her laptop was on the kitchen counter, so she picked it up and walked back to her room.

"Who is Lilith?" she typed into the search engine. An hour, two hours, and three hours passed as she read about Lilith, the demon. She found the following passage from Wikipedia particularly illuminating.

After God created Adam, who was alone, He said, "It is not good for man to be alone." He then created a woman for Adam from the earth, as He had created Adam himself, and called her Lilith. Adam and Lilith immediately began to fight. She said, "I will not lie below," and he said, "I will not lie beneath you, but only on top. For you are fit only to be in the bottom position, while I am to be the superior one." Lilith responded, "We are equal to each other inasmuch as we were both created from the earth." But they would not listen to one another. When Lilith saw this, she pronounced the Ineffable Name and flew away into the air.

Karma took a deep breath and remembered what Danielle had told her about being on top.

She continued reading.

...stories portray Lilith as a demoness who kills children and takes advantage of men while they are sleeping. Lilith uses men's seeds during masturbation and erotic dreams and uses them to replenish her own offspring.

The origins of Lilith are challenging to pinpoint as she transitions from a fertility goddess to a demon.

Karma felt her hands shaking. *Oh my god. Danielle is Lilith. Lilith is Danielle.*

A chill ran down Karma's spine. Raised in an Arab Christian family and educated in religion classes at her private Christian school, she had never heard of this Lilith figure. In her teachings, Adam had only one wife, Eve. Her Muslim friends also held the belief that it was Eve and only Eve. Karma began to question her religious upbringing. *Were we mistaken all this time? Did Eve have a counterpart, a nemesis? Eve versus Lilith. Just like me versus Danielle. Oh my, what have I gotten myself into?*

THAT NIGHT, KARMA asked Jamal if she could be on top.

"Really?" he asked, already on top of her. "Where did that come from?"

She blushed but also felt emboldened. "I don't know. I thought we could try something new."

Without skipping a beat, Jamal flipped her over so she was on top, and the minute that happened, she knew there was no going back. She felt she was transforming into Lilith, with an aura of red flames dancing around her. She felt in control of her man, of her life, of her sexual pleasure. When he slid quickly inside her, she had her first orgasm, an immense wave that ripped her insides. A second wave followed immediately as she bounced up and down while watching him climax. Her shrieks of pleasure were so loud that she thought her whole neighborhood might have heard her.

"Wow. That was amazing," said Jamal, still panting. "And very quick."

Karma rolled on her back and felt completely drained of energy, as if she had shed her older self. She fell asleep as soon as her head hit the pillow.

When Karma woke up the following day, she felt nauseous and ran to the bathroom, where she threw up. Everything hurt; even her boobs were sore.

Nausea. Vomiting. Sore breasts.

Wait a minute.

Danielle's words rushed through her head.

Am I pregnant?

Chapter 8

SHE LOOKED ONCE, closed her eyes, and opened them again. A blue line appeared, indicating a positive result.

It can't be right. It just can't. They told us we wouldn't get pregnant naturally, and IVF was our only chance.

She was seated on the toilet in the master bedroom, and her underwear was pulled down to her knees. The window was open, and she felt the crisp morning air of that fall day. She shivered.

They were sure about it. Aren't they supposed to be the best doctors in the world? How did they mess this up?

Karma didn't know what to think or how to feel.

How did I not notice this? Did I miss my period with all that mess? Jamal said we needed to schedule an IVF, and I told him I needed a few months' break. Is this when this happened? Did this break lead me to conceive?

Karma wondered if that demonic Danielle had messed with her hormones. Or maybe she had messed with her sense of time, making her forget to track her cycle.

Stop it, you're going crazy, she told herself.

Should she be happy, scared, or worried? Should she call her mom immediately and tell her? Or should she wait, just in case it was only a fluke? Maybe it was all in her head, and she imagined things.

She couldn't stop thinking about Danielle and what she told her about the baby. How did she know? Was it her talking, or was it that demon, Lilith, with that mature voice?

She took a deep breath and thought about her research the night before. Some sources portrayed Lilith as a fertility goddess, while others described her as the killer of babies.

Which one was Lilith? The killer or the goddess?

Possessively cradling her still normal-sized belly, Karma wondered whether Danielle was really possessed by the devil Lilith.

Believing in demonic possession was insane. The irony was not lost on Karma. She, of all people, should have been the first to believe in the supernatural and the unexplained, but she didn't. This was not a Hollywood movie. Karma's talent for seeing things before they happened was just a genetic mutation.

Karma caressed her stomach. She didn't feel a thing. No kicks, no heartbeats, no butterflies. She even hoped for a vision, something, but nothing.

Where were her visions when she needed them?

Karma sighed, wiped the pregnancy test clean, capped it, washed her hands, and then headed back to the bedroom. Jamal was awake, seated on the edge of the bed, putting on his socks.

She sat beside him in bed and showed him the blue line.

He squinted his eyes. "Oh, my God. Am I seeing what I think I'm seeing?"

"Yes," she said, a slight smile forming on her face.

"Holy shit! How?"

Her voice cracked. "I guess it just happened."

"I can't believe it! We're going to have a baby." He hugged Karma tightly. The touch and smell of him sparked her arousal; she ached for him to be inside of her. She needed that comfort. She needed the assurance that everything was still fine, that no stupid demons were chasing her.

"Man, this is the best day of my life," he said, then looked at Karma. "Are you okay? You don't look happy."

"I'm happy," she said with a smile. "Just worried."

He held her hand. "That's normal. Everything will be okay. We will have a healthy, beautiful baby just like you." He kissed her on the cheek. "We need to tell Dr. Grahm."

She nodded, then squeezed his hand. "I'll call him today. I promise."

He kissed her forehead. "Listen, I have a big surgery this morning. Don't make anything for dinner tonight. We're going to celebrate. We'll go to that Italian restaurant you like. Oregano's?"

"I would love that," she said and kissed him goodbye. "I love you," she whispered in his ear. She was not one who often said, "I love you." That time, though, she felt she had to say it. She needed to say it.

He smiled. "I love you, too."

WHEN KARMA TOLD her mom a few hours later, over FaceTime, her mom ululated. Lu-Lu-Lu-Leech! "I told you it'd work the natural way. You didn't have to take all that medicine and poison those American doctors stuffed you with," Karma's mom told her.

Karma rolled her eyes. "Alhamdulillah, it worked out."

"Alhamdulillah," her mom responded. "Have you picked a name yet? I have a feeling it's a boy."

"Not yet. We just found out a few hours ago. And I think Jamal is hoping for a girl."

"No, no. He's just saying that. All men want sons."

Karma sighed. "I need to walk the dog now."

"No, no, you don't walk the dog. You stay home, put your feet up, and rest. You let your husband walk the dog from now on. Or maybe you don't need a dog now that you will have a son."

Karma let out a sigh as if she couldn't handle walking her dog and having a baby. "Mama, what are you saying? I'll never give him up."

Her mom shook her head. "Uff! Just promise to stop walking him. I don't want you to tire yourself, especially during the first few months."

Karma didn't listen. As soon as she finished talking to her mom and got out of the house, she put a leash on Baladi. It was cold, and she had forgotten to bring a hat and gloves. She was still not accustomed to all the winter gear she had to gather before venturing outside. She felt the gust on her face as she looked up at the falling leaves. The cornucopia of fall colors lifted her spirits.

She put her hands in the pockets of her fleece jacket and looked at the piles of leaves gathered neatly on the side of the road. She watched an elderly neighbor rake leaves, probably rushing to collect as many as possible before the city leaf collection truck came to take them away.

Fall chores were new to her. Jamal had already hired someone to blow the leaves for them, as she had no idea where to start. There had been few trees where she grew up, and they were all evergreen.

Karma suddenly felt homesick. She missed her dad's Turkish coffee that he made for her and her mom every morning. Her son would grow up away from his grandparents. That thought made her teary. Her son wouldn't have what she had - walking to the open street market near her apartment building and getting hot falafel sandwiches for breakfast. The beeping of car horns, the Arabic music blasting from cars' radios, and kids running in the street until after midnight with no bedtime in sight - he would miss the chaos of it all.

She needed her mom.

She couldn't do this without her mom. She couldn't raise a baby on her own.

She sighed and placed her hand on her stomach, rubbing it in the hope of feeling something heartbeat, perhaps, or a tiny movement. Nothing occurred.

Am I even pregnant? Maybe the test is not accurate. What if Danielle had cursed my baby?

When Karma got home from walking Baladi, she went online and ordered the book What to Expect When You're Expecting from Amazon, then went to BabyCenter.com and read about the first trimester. She found herself being sucked into a rabbit hole of terror, everything that could go wrong, from miscarriages to birth defects to ectopic pregnancy.

Feeling nauseous, she closed the lid of her laptop. She bit her left thumbnail as she thought about the day ahead.

She missed Veronica and all the time they had spent together. She longed for a friend who knew what she was going through. She felt lonely, stuck in an old house with a demanding dog and an absent husband.

At least she had Jill.

She needed to check on her.

Crazy Danielle had made Karma forget all about her.

Karma went to her front porch and grabbed some lavender and Black-Eyed Susan before heading toward Jill's. When she stopped in front of her ranch-style house, she hesitated a bit. What was she going to say? Should she tell her about the pregnancy? She took a deep breath, then rang the bell.

When Jill opened the door, Karma noticed that she looked thin—thinner than when she had last seen her. She had a cast on her arm and appeared as if she hadn't slept in years. Her face was pale, her eyes hollow. She smiled when she saw Karma and thanked her for the flowers.

As Karma stepped inside, her gaze briefly caught a framed photograph on the mantle: Jill's daughter, a teenage girl with brown hair and a smile that lit up her whole face, her hazel eyes sparkling with joy. The contrast between the energetic child in the picture and Jill's weary figure was striking.

Jill's house was littered with old pieces of furniture shoved against the walls in the main room: a wicker chair, a round table, and a side table. The whole place smelled of wood varnish. Jill's dog came running to greet her. Karma petted her.

"Excuse the mess. I need to sell those pieces soon. Never have the time to do anything these days," said Jill as she opened the blinds. She motioned for Karma to sit in the middle on a brown leather sofa. Karma sat down, moving an empty Coca-Cola bottle to the side.

Jill sat at the far end of the sofa and turned her head toward Karma.

"How are you feeling?" asked Karma, tapping Jill's shoulder. She suddenly remembered that el Amreekan valued their personal space and didn't like to be touched without consent. She immediately pulled her hand back. *The last thing I need now is another vision with Jill in it.*

"I'm okay. Just in pain. A lot of pain," said Jill. "I'm glad you're here. Do you think Jamal can prescribe me something for the pain? My doctor is busy and keeps ignoring me."

Karma let out a long sigh. "Jill, I know," she said.

"You know what?" she said, narrowing her eyes.

Karma looked Jill straight in the eyes. "I know everything. I know about your addiction," she said, stressing the word addiction.

Jill bit her lip. "I don't know what you're talking about," she said.

"I know about Danielle. I knew she was responsible for this. Please stop denying this."

Jill's eyes filled with tears. "How? How do you know all of this?"

"I was there," said Karma. "I was there in the woods when it happened."

"You were?" How come you didn't help me?" Jill tilted her head.

"I wasn't in a position to help. Listen, I'm worried about you. You're my friend," said Karma.

Jill's dog Mia started barking.

"Shut up," shouted Jill at the dog. "Shut the fuck up!" She leaned her head in her hands and started sobbing. "You don't understand. I'm in a lot of pain. Doctors are refusing to prescribe me anything, and Danielle is my only hope."

Karma raised her eyebrows. "Danielle? Really? The one who broke your arm."

Jill wiped her tears. "We had a misunderstanding."

Mia began to bark again, so Jill sprang out of the sofa and whacked her forcefully on her back. Karma cringed as Jill smacked her dog. One time. Two times. Three times. The dog whimpered.

"Shut the fuck up, you stupid dog!"

Karma was aghast. So much for all that talk about adopting an unwanted three-legged dog and all of that. What a hypocrite. All of them are hypocrites, those self-righteous suburban moms who think they are making the world a better place and ranting on social media for people to do better. She opened her mouth to say something, to make Jill stop hitting that poor dog, but no words came out.

When Jill returned to where Karma was sitting and took a seat next to her, Karma mustered enough courage to continue the conversation. "What kind of misunderstanding did you have with Danielle?" she asked.

"It's complicated."

"Stop lying to yourself," Karma blurted. Shit. That was harsh.

Jill crossed her arms over her chest. "Seriously? Who are you to judge me?"

Karma bit her lower lip. "I'm sorry. I didn't mean it that way." She felt her phone buzzing in her jeans pocket. Probably, Jamal was checking in on her. *I would have to lie to him again.*

Jill's voice interrupted her thoughts. "How did you mean it? Because seriously, it was pretty bitchy."

"I care about you," she said, tapping Jill's shoulder and then pulling her hand away quickly.

"I think we're done here," said Jill and stood up. "I have shit to do."

Karma swallowed hard; her throat was tight. "I'm sorry. I just want you to be okay.

"Please leave," said Jill, pointing to the door with her shaky index finger.

Hitting Mia like this was just out of character. It's not like you. I know how much you love your dog."

KARMA WALKED HOME in tears, thinking about all the friendships that she had ruined. Veronica, now Jill. She wanted to disappear. She wanted the earth to open up and swallow her whole. Every bit of her. She felt she couldn't live anymore, while visions of other people's lives kept haunting her. Her life was one big fat lie. Even her marriage was a facade. Her husband didn't even know her true self and had no idea about her visions, all her thoughts, and all the lives she had shattered. And the baby? Would she ever reveal herself to him or her? What if her visions ruined that baby, messing with his infant brain?

She should not have children. Her kind were not meant to have children.

She should not even be allowed to live, to roam the earth freely.

She paused walking and looked around her neighborhood. The pretty houses, with their front lawns and big trees, featured driveways that often included basketball hoops. The smooth sidewalks were designed for moms to push their strollers and kids to ride their scooters. The air was crisp, and she felt it hit her face. Who did she think she was to belong in this place? To pretend that she was one of them. That she could live like them, be like them, with their backyard BBQs, their minivans, and their beach gateways.

No. I must live. I must live for this baby. I was given this baby for a reason.

When she arrived at her house, she unlocked the front door, tears streaming down her cheeks. She sniffled, then suddenly felt a cold whiff of air and shivered. She heard heavy breathing and smelled a strong scent of rosewater. She turned around to find herself face-to-face with Danielle.

She shrieked. A vision began to take shape before her.

Karma was six. She was swimming in a pool in Bilaq. It was a sweltering day, and the pool was packed. Her friend Noor challenged her to jump off the diving board. She was a bit hesitant. She had never jumped off the board. She had a secret. She didn't know how to swim. Usually, she would just splash around the water and hang on the edge, but when Noor challenged her and teased her, she had no choice but to jump off the board. She would just jump near the edge and quickly hang on. When Karma got to the board and looked down, she felt dizzy. As she was about to jump, Noor ran behind her and pushed her, making her fall into the middle of the pool. She tried to move her arms and legs to float, but she couldn't. She tried until her arms and legs gave up. She felt herself drowning. This is it, she thought. As she was slipping under the water, a boy came out of nowhere. He swam toward her, grabbed her arm, then carried her on her back and swam with her toward the edge. When she got out of the pool, she looked for the boy and couldn't find him.

"Hey, hey, relax. It's only me," said Danielle, smiling. "You need to take it easy, you know. You gotta listen to your mom." She touched Karma's belly, making circular motions with her hand.

Karma stepped back, her head bumping against the wooden front door.

"What do you want from me? Don't touch me," she said in between sobs. Karma wanted to get inside her house immediately and escape the witch.

"Why all that crying?" Danielle said sweetly, wiping a strand of hair off Karma's forehead and tucking it behind her ear.

Karma stood very still, trying to will herself to think a happy thought. But that damn rosewater was all her senses could latch on to.

Danielle squared her shoulders. "Come on, Karma. You know you're special, unique, a visionary. Now get these dark thoughts out of your head and focus on what's coming next."

"Go away!" hissed Karma, summoning the courage to speak. She would not let this demon around her baby.

Danielle looked her up and down, that sick smile still on her face. "Hey, hey, I told you to take it easy. Don't let those pregnancy hormones mess with your head, and don't waste your time trying to save that loser, Jill. She's a lost cause. A goner. I told you... You can't change fate. Just focus on yourself now."

Danielle took a step closer. Karma could smell her breath, which smelled like rotten eggs. She felt queasy. "Fuck off!" shouted Karma, surprising herself by uttering such a nasty word.

Danielle's irises slowly started to turn red, and her breath became heavy. "Don't you anger me now," she warned, her voice changing to a more mature tone, hoarser and deeper.

Karma shivered.

Danielle grabbed Karma's arm and clenched it with her fist. Karma felt excruciating pain in her forearm, right where Danielle's fingers dug in mercilessly. "Leave Jill alone. She's mine now. Don't mess with what's mine, and focus on what's yours."

"I already told your mom all about what you are doing," Karma said through trembling lips. "She knows about the drugs and everything."

Danielle cackled. "My mom? You foolish girl, you! Do you even know the amount of drugs my mom steals from that hospital where she works? You're so dumb. She'll be discovered soon and will rot in prison like all the other drug dealers."

Karma couldn't breathe. Was Danielle messing with her head? She didn't know who she should trust anymore in this crazy neighborhood, in this crazy country.

Danielle tapped with her index finger on Karma's sweaty forehead. "My advice: focus instead on that perfect husband of yours. You never know where his eyes may wander."

With a flourish, she released Karma's arm, turned around, and walked away. Halfway down the walkway, she stopped, turned her head, and said with a smile, "Remember, you can't escape Karma."

SCARED, DEPRESSED, AND worried about Danielle's threats, Karma spent the next few weeks in bed, nauseous and tired. Even her breasts ached.

She threw up nonstop and felt weak and dehydrated. The world was not a wonderful place to be in. She didn't feel any attachment to the baby growing inside her. She didn't experience any glow or bliss or any maternal instinct, the mommy bloggers kept talking about. She felt empty, devoid of any sort of joy. Everything around her was bleak.

"It's okay, babe," Jamal told her over the phone when she called him crying. "All women feel this way in the first trimester. You'll wake up in the second trimester, and you'll have that mom-to-be glow you keep reading about."

Karma feared Danielle had cursed her and the baby. Karma had messed with Danielle's plan, telling her mom about her and confronting Jill. Danielle would never leave her alone. And the baby, her baby, was the easiest target. She wished that the witch would return to hell, where she came from.

JAMAL WAS AS helpful a husband as Karma could dream of. While he still had to work long hours at the hospital to help her rest and stay in bed, he ordered food and hired a neighbor to walk the dog. He also hired cleaners to tidy up the house twice a week.

"I already spoke with Dr. Grahm," said Jamal, sitting on the edge of the bed and holding Karma's hand in his. "He assured me that you're fine and that some pregnancies are just extremely unpleasant in the beginning, and it seems you're one of those people." He squeezed her hand. "You know, it will be good for you to walk a bit every day. It's not healthy to stay in bed all the time. You don't want to develop a blood clot, God Forbid."

"Things don't seem right," said Karma, sitting on the bed with a breakfast tray on her lap. An image of Danielle grabbing her wrist flashed before her eyes.

"Come on, honey," he said, stroking her jawline. "This is your first pregnancy. You're not used to all these new feelings with all the hormones. We've already seen the doctor; he checked you and the baby. Everything is fine."

"I hope so," she said, tears rolling down her cheeks.

"Trust me," he said, wiping away her tears. "You'll be okay. We will have a healthy, beautiful baby."

He had so much hope in his brown eyes that it broke her heart. How could she stand it if she let him down?

"I can't stop crying these days," she wept.

"It's okay, baby. It's just the hormones."

On Thanksgiving Day, Jamal ordered a ready-made meal from Whole Foods, placed it on a tray, and brought it to Karma in bed. They both ate silently as Jamal watched a football game on TV.

"You know, I never grew up eating turkey on Thanksgiving," he told her.

"Really?" she asked. "What did you eat?"

"My mom always insisted on making lamb. She thought turkey was tasteless."

"She's right," said Karma, smiling.

He leaned his head against her shoulder. "There was always lamb and rice with pine nuts."

Karma inhaled the scent of her husband. He smelled of cologne and soap. "Now that sounds delicious," she said.

WHEN KARMA FELT a bit better a couple of weeks later, she decided to venture outside. She missed her walks with Baladi and missed chatting with the neighbors. After a long shower, she wore jeans, a V-neck white sweater, and brown leather boots. She even put on some makeup after weeks of neglecting herself. She wanted to look good, feel good, and forget about Danielle, Jill, and all the craziness around the neighborhood.

It was a chilly December morning, and the air was dry. She remembered to grab all the cold-weather gear—gloves, a sweater, and a hat. There was no bad weather, only bad clothes—she'd read that somewhere.

She walked Baladi as she marveled at the Christmas decorations. She, too, wanted to decorate her house. Growing up as a Christian in an apartment in Bilaq, her family had a fake Christmas tree that her mom decorated every year with red plastic balls and a few broken ornaments. On Christmas Day, her parents gave her an envelope with 50 dollars. That was pretty much it. They didn't have a house or a yard to decorate, nor did they have the means to put up outdoor lights. Would Jamal have time to go all out as she wanted? Maybe they could hire a handyman. She wanted to have the lights, the deer, the snowman, the tree, the wreath, the candy canes, the nutcrackers, and all the festive decorations she had seen in the American movie National Lampoon's Christmas Vacation.

This was her life now.

It was not a movie.

It was her reality.

As for her dark thoughts during the past few weeks, she was wrong. She wanted to live. To experience joy. To be a mother. To hold her baby in her hands. To breastfeed.

There was still so much to live for.

Danielle couldn't take these things away from her.

At home, she looked at the pile of mail the cleaners neatly put on the white leather chair near the door: Amazon and USPS boxes, junk mail, and bills. She went through all the items she had ordered and forgotten about during her time in bed: a pair of white gloves, a new Kindle, a new harness for Baladi, dog treats, and a dog winter sweater.

She opened a box that had a return address in China. Had she, in her delirium, ordered something from China?

Inside the box was a black belt; attached to it was what looked like a plastic male organ.

Oh, my God. Did Jamal order this? Worse, did he expect to use it with her? Was he watching some sort of kinky porn? What could he be thinking? She was pregnant! Sex was the last thing on her mind!

She flipped the box and then breathed a sigh of relief. It was addressed to Gina Kopp, who lived two doors down. The mail carrier must have dropped it at their house by mistake.

Gina? Of all people? Was she into this stuff? Gina, the career-oriented single CEO who was hardly home? Did she even have time to date?

Gina had a large nose and harsh features. Her voice was coarse from all the smoking. She was not particularly popular on her street, and Karma had heard some neighbors refer to her as "unfriendly" and "stuck-up." She always seemed alone and bitter. Once, Karma had seen her yell at a neighborhood kid for jumping in her leaf pile.

Karma taped the box back, put a leash on Baladi, grabbed the box, and went outside. She had to get rid of the box before Jamal got home, as she was sure he would tell her to throw it away immediately. Karma didn't feel it was the right thing to do; she had to return the box to where it belonged. Gina wouldn't be home. She would be at work or traveling the world, signing international financial deals.

At Gina's house, as expected, there was no car in the driveway. Karma calmly walked to the front door and dropped off the box on the front step. As she was about to turn around and head home, the front door opened, and Gina emerged, dressed in gray sweatpants and a blue T-shirt that said "Cornell." Her brown hair was tied up in a bun.

Karma's heart dropped, and she felt her cheeks flush.

"Hi," said Gina.

"Um, hi, the mailman dropped this box by mistake at our house," said Karma, pointing to the box on the front step. "I was just returning it." Karma had difficulty forming a coherent sentence, feeling like she had lost the ability to speak English.

Gina leaned down and picked up the box. "I see," she said, looking up at Karma and smiling. "My car is in the shop, so I'm working from home today."

Karma felt her cheeks burning. Would Gina know she'd opened it? How would she ever face this woman again?

Gina took a step toward Karma and touched her shoulder. "Thank you," she whispered.

Suddenly, an image flashed in front of Karma's eyes. Gina was naked.

No, no. Karma didn't want to see this. Yuck. Yuck. Stop. Happy memories. Happy memories. Beach. Sunrise. Baladi. Christmas lights. Falafel Sandwiches, Turkish coffee. Stop. Stop.

The image didn't stop.

Gina, naked, straddling a man. She moved up and down, riding him like a cowgirl. The man was moaning. She was moaning.

"You're so sexy," said the man between his moans.

"And you're so hot. I can do this all day. God, you're so hot."

Karma saw the man's features: black hair and soft skin. Her heart dropped, and she let out a shriek.

Jamal.

Karma sprinted home and settled on the sofa, then let out a wail. She felt her hands tremble, and then everything in her body hurt, and she felt exhausted. Lying down, she drifted into a deep sleep for hours, maybe days, until she lost count. She imagined she was on a beach, sipping a cocktail. She imagined wearing a red bikini and reading a book on a lounge chair, the sun warming her skin. She closed her eyes and could almost hear the sound of the ocean.

When she opened her eyes, Jamal was standing in front of her, staring at her. He was wearing navy blue swim trunks. His bare chest showed unusually toned abs. He leaned in and kissed her on the mouth. She pulled him toward her and kissed him back. He climbed on top of her and pushed his tongue inside her mouth. She got a tingling between her legs, and she kept on kissing him. She felt a metallic taste in her mouth, and she let go of him. She wiped her mouth and looked at her hands. Blood. She looked at him; instead of his face, there was the face of a stranger, an older man with rugged features and a crooked nose. The man was bleeding everywhere, from his mouth, his eyes, and his nose. He growled. More blood came out of his mouth and splashed on her face.

She woke up screaming.

Baladi barked. She got out of the sofa, rushed to the bathroom, and threw up.

When Jamal came home that night, he asked her if she needed anything, but she pretended to be asleep. He covered her with a blanket, kissed her on the cheek, and whispered goodnight in her ear.

"Hypocrite," she whispered to herself as he went upstairs to the bedroom.

SHE DIDN'T LEAVE the house for weeks. She spent most of her days sleeping on the sofa downstairs. She didn't want to wake up and face him. Part of her wanted him to perish. The pain was unbearable. Her heart was broken into one million pieces, and each piece felt like a sharp knife penetrating her ribs. She couldn't breathe.

She kept replaying the vision in her mind. That vision. The one with him with that bitch, cunt, whore—Gina. She is on top of him. Both of them were moaning in pleasure.

Yuck, yuck, yuck.

When had they done it? When he'd told her he had an "emergency" surgery late at night? How many times had he lied to her? Where had they met? In her house? At a cheap hotel?

How many times had they fucked? Was it once? A one-night stand thing? Were they having a full-fledged affair? Had they fornicated once, twice, dozens, hundreds of times?

What if this vision is wrong—a hallucination because of the pregnancy hormones? What if Danielle really messed with my mind? No, no. My visions are never wrong. He did it. He is doing it. He is a cheater. What a cliché. I'm married to a cheater, just like in a daytime soap opera. Cliches exist for a reason because they happen in real life. My life.

She didn't want to see his face. She just wanted to spit at him. To shove him, to slap him, to shred him to pieces. To cut his organ off and feed it to Baladi.

What did he see in Gina? Was it the fact that she was not Karma? That she was a hotshot CEO who traveled the world signing deals? That she was empowered and independent? That he didn't need him to show her the ropes of American life? He didn't have to educate her to be an American. He'd picked her because she was the complete opposite of his demure immigrant wife.

During those weeks of her confinement on the sofa, she hardly did anything around the house. Jamal brought food daily and occasionally did the laundry.

"Are you sure you're okay?" he would ask.

She would nod and switch the channel or pretend to be asleep. Alternatively, she would turn her back on him, feigning fatigue.

She wanted to sleep and forget. About everything. About her disgusting, vile, cheating husband. About that ugly whore Gina, about that freak Danielle, about Baladi, and even about the baby. She ate little, and when she was awake, she would watch some trashy TV and fall asleep.

She had weird aches and pains. Pain in her stomach, in her pelvis. She had headaches, and the nausea never abated. She didn't want that baby anymore. She didn't want anything as evidence that Jamal had been inside her, not his baby, not his penis. Nothing.

She loathed him. All the sacrifices she'd made for him, leaving her family, her country, her friends, her backbone, just to be with him, a cheater. A cheater who threw her into a boring suburb where people were cold and distant, with significant mental illnesses.

She switched between wanting to die and wanting to live long enough to get revenge. To cause him even more pain than he had caused her.

"I'm worried about you," her mom said over FaceTime. "You haven't been returning my calls, and you look awful. Are you losing weight?"

"I'm just tired." She let out a big sigh and got quiet.

"Is everything okay with the baby?" Karma's mom said, sounding worried.

"Yes. The doctor said everything looks okay, and I should start gaining weight soon."

Karma's mom softened. "Just rest, habeebti. Your husband is rich. He can afford to buy you food every day and hire cleaners."

She paused, the brief silence on the line heavy. "Yup. That's what he's doing."

"Do you want me to come and stay with you? I can come now. I can take the next flight." Karma could hear her mom calling for her husband. "I'm going to America to see Karma," she told him.

Karma could hear some commotion over FaceTime. Maybe her dad was bringing her mom her afternoon Turkish coffee.

"You're going to America? When?" she heard her dad say. "You're just telling me now!"

"No, Mama, stop," said Karma, annoyed. "Stop it. No one is coming to America. Just wait until the baby arrives. That's when I'll need the most help,"

"Are you sure you're okay?" her mom asked.

That's when Karma broke down and started crying.

"What is it? What's the matter? Why are you crying?"

Karma struggled to find her voice. "I'm worried Jamal is cheating on me."

Karma heard her mom sigh, and then she got silent. "Mama, are you there?"

"Yeah, I'm here."

"Did you hear me?

"Yeah, I did, silly girl," her mom said. "Is that it? Is that the only thing bothering you? Don't you know... all men cheat. That's who they are. That's how God made them. Didn't I teach you that already?"

Fresh tears filled Karma's eyes. Not her Baba, too. "What are you saying? Baba cheated on you?"

Her mom made a tsk noise. "I don't know, and I don't care. It's not a big deal. He's a good husband and a good provider. He can't help being a man. That's how God made him. Men are wired this way. They must spread their seed everywhere."

"I can't believe you think it's okay! I'll never be fine with Jamal cheating. Never!" Karma said, her voice grew louder.

"Really, Karma? Really?" her mom said, almost shouting. "Are you turning into one of those Americans who believe in love and lifetime loyalty and all of that? These are all fantasies—lies they sell to you, lies they tell you in their Hollywood movies."

"Mom, I have to go," said Karma as she ended the phone call.

After that call, Karma didn't call her mom for at least another week. She needed a break. Her mom tried to call several times, but Karma never picked up. She had had enough.

BY THE END of her first trimester, Karma started to feel better. Christmas had come and gone, and Karma hadn't done anything special. One afternoon, she woke up from her nap, and just like that, the nausea, aches, and pains were gone. She felt energetic, happy, and even.

Is this the "glow" they talk about in pregnancy books?

She took a long shower, applied some makeup, and got dressed in black tights, a red, long-sleeved tunic, black boots, a black parka, and a black beanie. Jamal can go fuck himself. At least he gave her a baby, and that was what mattered.

She put Baladi on a leash and ventured outside on a cold winter day. She marveled at the bare trees stripped of their leaves and the quiet streets. She sniffed the smell of burning firewood wafting from the neighbors' fireplaces and felt a big smile grow on her face.

She thought about an article she read about the Danish way of embracing winter: Hygge. Maybe she should adopt a more Danish approach this winter. She would turn on the fireplace, light candles, drink hot cocoa, and snuggle under a throw blanket. She would read a book by the fire and think about her future with the baby, a future without her cheating, lying husband.

She looked at some of the neighbors' yard signs she came across during her walk. Some endorsed candidates for local elections, and others sent political and social messages about tolerance and accepting people of all kinds. She found it fascinating that Americans felt the need to be vocal and to voice their opinions on various issues. There were surveys, polls, yard signs, and bumper stickers.

In Bilaq, people were scared. Voicing your opinion, especially your political views, could get you in trouble. There would always be someone listening and reporting you to the authorities. Ears and eyes were everywhere. In Bilaq, people kept their opinions to themselves. No one blasted them on their front yards.

She walked and thought about her life and the options presented before her. Would she leave Jamal? Would she become a single mom who worked three jobs? Would she go back to Bilaq and be labeled mutallaqa, a divorced woman? Or would she raise her child in the US, where he or she would have a better future? However, in Bilaq, she had a strong support system: her mom, her dad, her friends, her cousins, and her whole community, who thought like her, talked like her, behaved like her, and looked like her, making her feel like an insider rather than an outsider.

She had no clue what to do.

When she got home, she noticed a package outside her front door. She was not expecting any packages that day. Not again! Another toy for Gina, the bitch!

She picked it up. It was addressed to her, Karma Ibrahim. She looked for the sender's name, but there was nothing there, just a P.O. Box number from Bilaq.

A box from Bilaq? Who would have sent it? She knew her mom never trusted the mail, and all the stuff she had sent Karma before was hand-delivered through friends or family members who were traveling to the US.

She flipped the box, shook it, and heard a faint thumping sound.

Once inside, she let Baladi lounge on the living room sofa. Then, she went to the kitchen, grabbed a pair of scissors, and cuddled up next to Baladi.

She tore the box open with the scissors and looked inside.

Three notebooks of different sizes, all with faded brown leather covers. She picked the first one and ran her fingers across it. She sniffed it. It smelled of dust.

She flipped through the worn-out yellow pages. The writing was in Arabic in fading blue ink. It looked like a young person's writing, perhaps a kid or a teenager, and there was a vague sense of familiarity to the handwriting that she couldn't quite grasp. When was this written? She flipped through the pages again. There were no dates anywhere.

Is this a journal?

Karma took off her brown Timberland shoes, the ones she'd bought after seeing an ad on Instagram, and her socks and lay across the sofa. She picked a random page from the journal and started reading.

Malik is harassing me. I hate that fat boy, I hate him, I hate him. Since he found out about me, about that thing in me, he has not stopped bothering me. He waits for me when I leave the apartment and starts calling me el jenyeeh, the witch, the evil woman.

I hate him. He is so ugly and mean and fat, and I wish he would disappear from the face of the earth. He even told his ugly brother, Iyad, about me, and now both of them follow me on my way to the store and shout.

"El jenyeeh! El jenyeeh!"

I'm stupid. So stupid. I should not have told him about that thing. I really didn't mean to. I just blurted it out. I told him that the crazy lady who lives down the street, who wanders barefoot and throws her flip-flops at her children, would be stabbed by her husband after they fight over the magloubeh she would make for dinner, which he would think was overcooked and dry.

When that happened, Malik was the first to tell me. He knocked on the door of our apartment building, and as soon as I opened it, he called me el Jenyeeh, ifrite—the daughter of Satan.

When I asked him to stop and asked why he was mean, he told me the crazy lady had died. Her husband stabbed her, just like I told him it would happen.

"How did you know, ya jenyeeh? How did you even know she would cook magloubeh that night?" he asked me.

I told him I just knew things. He shoved me, and I fell on the floor.

Now, he follows me around all over the neighborhood, and I run away whenever I see him and his fat brother, Iyad. Mama told me to ignore them, that they are stupid, fat, ugly kids, that they are not worth my time, and that I should keep my mouth shut.

Zip it, just zip it.

Karma gasped. Baladi, who was resting next to her, lifted his head and licked her bare foot. What was this journal? Who did it belong to? Why had it been sent to her? How did they know where she lived?

Was there another person out there from Bilaq who had visions, too? And they knew about her? Who could that be? She thought of all the people she'd told about her visions growing up: Arwa, her neighbor, and one kid from the neighborhood. Did they still remember? Did they find this journal and send it to her? Why? To scare her? Karma flipped manically through the pages with her trembling fingers and settled on another page.

I can't breathe. I want to die. Please, God, kill me. I can't live this way. I can't anymore. It was a child this time. It was my cousin Inas. I saw it. I saw it when she hugged me at Isa's wedding. Why would I get this vision this time? This was not the first time I hugged her. Why now? I saw her being hit by the car. I saw her being thrown to the floor. Then I saw her in the hospital. Then, I saw her in a wheelchair. Not reacting. Not moving. Tubes are coming out of her mouth. She looked dead but alive, out of this world. Gone but still breathing. Is this the life that is awaiting her? This beautiful, sweet six-year-old will soon be like the living dead. Oh God, oh God, please don't do this to her. Why her? Why? Please take me instead. I'm the evil one. Not Inas! I'm the one who should be hit by a car. I'm El Jenyeeh. The daughter of Satan.

Karma clenched her jaw so hard she heard it pop. She flipped to another page.

I stayed in bed all day today, as it was the first day of my period. My mom was happy, ululating and telling the next-door neighbor that I had just become a woman. "I was worried," Mama told me. "It took you so long. I thought there was something wrong with you."

Really, Mama. You, of all people, should know that there is something wrong with me. The last thing you should be worried about is my period. I'm not normal, Mama. I'm not normal. I'm not normal.

Karma felt dizzy. This was so familiar. Everything hit close to home. Karma heard Jamal's car roll up the driveway.

She stuffed all the journals back into the box and ran upstairs to their bedroom. The first place she thought of was under the bed. She retrieved all the journals from the box and, with her other hand, lifted the heavy bed mattress, spreading the journals underneath it.

He'd never find them. It wasn't like he ever changed the sheets.

She broke down the box quickly as she heard Jamal open the door. She lifted the mattress and stuffed it there next to all the journals.

Chapter 9

KARMA'S HEAD WAS spinning.

The journal!

Who? What? When?

What in God's name was going on? Who had tracked her down? Was someone trying to blackmail her? Maybe they assumed she was rich because she was married to a doctor. Should she call her mom and tell her? No, no. Her mom would lose her mind if she found out that her secret was out there, that other people really knew about the real her. She would worry Jamal would find out and divorce her—her mom's ultimate nightmare.

Karma went to bed that night with a million thoughts in her head, and for a while, she forgot about that asshole husband of hers who was screwing the neighbor, but when she woke up the next morning and saw his face, she felt nauseous, and she just wanted to die just like that person in the journal. She, too, was el Jenyeeh that needed to disappear.

She flipped through the journal the next day, searching for answers.

I had always thought that my first kiss would be wonderful, like explosions and fireworks. However, it was not. It was dull, and I wish it had never happened. As soon as his dry, chapped lips touched mine, I saw him as an older man. Maybe in his fifties, begging another man who looked like he could be his brother for money.

"Come on, Hatem, I just need four hundred to pay the rent," he pleaded.

"Why don't you get a job like the rest of us?" his ugly brother told him.

"Please, Hatem. I have a family."

"We all have families. Get a job and stop begging for money. I've given you more than enough."

When I saw that vision, I felt disgusted. I never want to be with a man like this. A man who can never provide. We were hiding under a tree behind our apartment building. I suddenly felt like throwing up, and the falafel he had for dinner didn't help. I quickly ran away and went home.

I will never find a man.

She put the journal aside. The stories were agitating her. That person who seemed to have the same condition as her and had sent her that journal was absolutely miserable. Was that what awaited Karma? Misery after misery? Her condition, her ability to see visions, was not a talent; it was a curse that would follow her for the rest of her life.

Karma had had enough of these journals.

She decided to take a long walk just to forget and maybe to disappear in the suburban streets, to turn into one of those aging trees planted in people's yards, rooted there for ages, never moving, never bothering anyone. Just aging quietly, gracefully, until one day, they would wither and get cut down, chopped into little pieces of wood. The cycle of life.

"Look what the cat brought in," said Danielle, who appeared out of nowhere on the corner of Spotwood Drive, interrupting Karma's train of thought. Danielle was wearing black leggings with her red Converse shoes that she never seemed to take off. Karma's heart skipped a beat at the sight of her, so she tugged Baladi's leash and turned around.

"Don't run away from me," she said, walking toward Karma. "I'm here to help you."

The smell of rosewater filled Karma's nostrils, so she started to walk faster. She didn't want to faint in the middle of the sidewalk.

"Don't waste your tears on that cheating husband of yours. It's now time to focus on yourself."

How did Danielle know? What kind of creature was she?

Karma stopped and turned around. "What do you want from me? Stop following me around."

"Girl, I'm trying to help you," said Danielle, smiling.

Karma raised her eyebrows. "Help me? Bullshit! You're the one who needs help. You're insane!"

"Hey, hey, no need to insult me," she said, throwing her hands in the air. "I'm here to give you advice."

Karma rolled her eyes. "Advice! From you? So I end up like Dom? Hanging from a rope, or like Jill with a broken arm, or going crazy like Veronica?"

Danielle shook her head. She pulled a black vape from the side pocket of her leggings and inhaled. "You really think I hurt Dom?"

How is she doing this out in public? Isn't she too young to smoke? Karma suddenly thought of that woman in the journal, and she wondered if she, too, had her own Danielle. Was there also a crazy witch following her around, taunting her?

"You foolish woman! I saved Dom. Next year, he would've died from leukemia."

Karma took a step back. "Really? And how do you know that? And if it was true, you just decided to steal whatever remaining life he had left? Why?"

Danielle locked eyes with Karma. "He didn't even know he had leukemia. We told him how he could escape his fate! The only way to beat your fate, to cheat it, is to end your life. This way, you can control your destiny. He'll come back and will lead a better life."

Why is she saying we? Who is the other person?

Karma took another step back. "So now you believe in reincarnation. You should go to prison for what you did to him."

"You should know by now that you are not the only one who sees visions. I was hoping those journals would help you get some perspective, but apparently not. He would've died ten months from now if we hadn't saved him."

How the fuck does she know about the journals? Maybe she was the one who sent them? "Please get some help," said Karma. "You need to be admitted to a mental institution. Helping Dom? Yeah, right. He and his mother didn't get a chance to say goodbye. There are effective treatments for leukemia. He could have beaten it. And how about Jill? Ha? How did you help her? By breaking her arm?"

Danielle rolled her eyes. "Jill was a lost cause. She needed a shock in her system to make her snap out of her misery. Last I heard, she had already checked herself into rehab. She wouldn't have done this if we hadn't shown her the dangerous world of addiction and drug dealers."

Jill is in rehab. Who is taking care of her daughter or her dog? "You separated Jill from her daughter. Do you think you did the right thing?"

Danielle waved her vape in the air. "Do you think she was much of a mom to her daughter? Really? She'll be a better one when she returns, when she's sober and attentive."

Where's the rehab center? Maybe I should visit her. "I don't believe you. I don't believe anything you say. What do you want from me?"

"I told you. I want to help you."

"Help me? How?"

Danielle got closer and put her hand on Karma's belly. Karma took a step back. A vision began to form in her mind.

Karma's mom is running on the beach barefoot, tears streaming down her face, her red dress flowing in the wind.

"Karma, Karma. We thought we lost you. We thought the ocean had swallowed you."

"I'm here, Mama. I was just collecting shells."

"Don't ever do this to me again. Don't disappear like that!"

Her mom hugged and wailed. That was the first time she had seen her mom emotional. Her mom, the rock of her life, was torn into pieces at the thought of losing her. Her mom did indeed love her. That was the first time she realized it.

Karma shook her head, willing the vision to disappear.

Danielle stared at her. "A healthy little boy you have here," she said.

"A boy?" Karma couldn't help but smile. Deep down, she knew her mom would be happy about a baby boy. Everyone in Bilaq would be pleased about the boy. She couldn't care less what Jamal thought.

"Yes. All is well with him," said Danielle while making circular motions around Karma's belly. "He'll be strong, powerful. Now, focus on yourself. Stop sulking and start living. It's your time." She smiled, showing her very white teeth.

"What are you saying exactly?" asked Karma.

She inhaled from her vape and then let out a cloud of smoke. "It's time to experience joy. There are a lot of handsome, nice men in this neighborhood. Enjoy your body, make connections, and have fun for a change. Don't be miserable. Don't be like that woman in the journal."

Karma threw her head back. "Are you crazy? I'm pregnant."

Danielle shook her head, "So fucking what? It's now the best time to do it. You are about to enter your second trimester. Soon, you will be so horny you won't be able to control yourself. Are you going to satisfy your needs with that cheating husband of yours? Or are you going to buy yourself a special toy like a typical deprived suburban wife? No. It's time for you to live and be happy. Trust me. Your happiness is the best revenge."

Danielle took a step closer and touched Karma's shoulder. Shivers ran up and down Karma's spine, and goose bumps began to crawl all over her skin.

"Why should I listen to you?" asked Karma. "You, of all people," she said, pointing her index finger at her. "You! The dog killer, the bone crusher, the bitch from hell."

"Well, because sometimes, honey, you must make a deal with the devil." Danielle smiled slyly before turning and walking away.

Karma couldn't stop thinking about what Danielle had told her. Revenge. Happiness. Hormones. Uncontrollable sexual urges.

I should not listen to her. She's crazy. She should be institutionalized. She's the voice of the devil. El Sheitan.

But then things changed rather rapidly. For the first time, Karma started to notice men, really notice them, like the young man with dreadlocks who regularly walked his white husky down her street during lunchtime. She had never paid him attention, but now she was subtly checking him out. The thought of running her hand on his toned, tanned muscles was scary but exhilarating.

Danielle had poisoned my thoughts.

Her eyes opened to the sight of all the men around her. She found herself looking at the guys in her neighborhood, at the grocery stores, and at the library. Men, handsome men, were everywhere.

A young man with blond hair who showed up at her doorstep to sell her new windows aroused her to a level she had never experienced before. She was lost in his blue eyes as he explained the pricing of the new window installation. She then noticed his muscular, toned arms. He must lift weights.

When he noticed her ogling him, he asked her where she was from.

She leaned by the side of the door and said, "Guess?" The burning sensation between her legs was immense.

He smiled. "Iranian?"

"Close," she said, her voice almost a whisper.

He grinned, showing his very white teeth. "Well, if you wanna meet up, give me a call. My name is Brent."

Brent, Brent, what kind of a name is Brent?

He handed her his card, and she deliberately brushed his hand against hers. "I'm interested, for sure," she said in a voice she didn't recognize as her own. She hoped for a vision at the touch of his skin, but nothing came. Instead, the urge to be touched by him was overwhelming.

As soon as he left, she went upstairs and touched herself. She thought of Brent as she climaxed, feeling the multiple waves of pleasure pulsating across her body.

That was the first time she had ever touched herself. She'd grown up being told it was filthy, dirty, and flat-out wrong.

Mama was wrong.

Masturbation was heavenly.

Her fantasies found their way to her dreams. Every night, she had dirty, steamy dreams. The men in her dreams were blondes and black-haired. Dark-skinned and light-skinned. Tall and short. Glasses and no glasses. Skinny and chubby. Fit and flabby. The dreams usually start with instant attraction, followed by sweet, sweet love. She was on top. He was on top. Sideways. On the kitchen counter. On the sofa. In the back seat of a car. On the beach. In the woods. She'd never had such vivid dreams and would wake up panting, sweating, and with an irresistible urge to touch herself, but she couldn't do that right next to sleeping Jamal. Sometimes, she would reach out to him as he snored beside her to feel his manhood. She didn't want him as a husband. She only wanted his body. His body would satisfy her for now.

She would try to go back to sleep, but she couldn't. Instead, she would spend hours looking at social media feeds and marveling at her friends'

Instagram posts. Some were married, and some were single. She envied them. Yes, life was not easy in Bilaq, but at least they had each other, unlike here, where she was alone, frustrated, with a cheating husband and a crazy demon stalking her.

As she walked Baladi around the neighborhood, she felt ashamed of her dreams and desires. Some of the men she'd fantasized about were her neighbors and dog walkers she'd occasionally interacted with. Married, single, engaged, in relationships—her dreams didn't make any distinction. Her dreams didn't care. All men were up for grabs.

What kind of person have I become? Lusting over random men like a sharmouta—a whore!

She passed by Steve, the neighbor on Maple Drive, as he took his usual daily jog. She smiled, and he smiled back. Her heart skipped a beat; Steve had been in her dream just the night before.

"Nice day, huh?" said Steve as he continued jogging.

"Gorgeous," she said, and she meant it. January was unusually warm, in the fifties, and sunny.

She replayed the dream of him caressing her nipples, igniting a stirring between her legs. Stop it. This is insane.

She kept walking until she passed Vadim, a neighbor on Hogwood Road, the street behind her house. He was outside, smoking a cigarette and leaning against the red Jeep parked in his driveway. He was wearing blue jeans and a blue turtleneck. His wavy, reddish hair was disheveled as if he had just woken up. His reddish beard was neatly trimmed. At first glance, he looked like one of those European cologne models.

As she passed by him, she smiled.

He threw the butt of his cigarette on the ground and asked, "How is your dog doing?"

As soon as he said that, Baladi jumped on his chest and started licking him. Vadim motioned to him to sit by making a fist, then lifting his hand and saying, "Sit."

Baladi immediately sat down and wagged his tail.

"Wow, he listened to you. You're good with dogs," said Karma as she struggled to pull Baladi's leash toward her.

"Yeah, I owned a couple of dogs back home," he said, running his hand through his reddish hair.

She smiled. "Not anymore?"

"Nah! I can't now. My wife is allergic," he said while patting Baladi.

"Your wife, Amanda?" she said, adjusting her posture and lifting her chest, her eyes meeting his.

"You know her?" he asked, cocking his head.

"Yeah. She works at the library, no?"

He nodded. "Yep. That's her."

"Oh, wow. She's very nice. She always recommends great books."

He laughed as he continued to pet Baladi. "Yeah. She reads nonstop. Sometimes, she forgets about us here and gets lost in her books."

Karma smiled. "I do that, too. So, do you have any tips on dog training?"

He rubbed his face, his fingertips gently pressing against his forehead and temples before sweeping down to massage his cheeks and perfect jawline as he tried to gather his thoughts. "Just make sure to teach him that you're the boss, and don't ever let him take charge."

She laughed. "Yeah. That's a good tip. You know, I never hired a trainer; maybe I should consider hiring one."

"Nah. Save your money. He seems like a nice dog; you can easily train him yourself," he said, then put his hand in his pocket and pulled a pack of Marlboro Lights. He lit a cigarette.

Ha! A chain smoker. Just like the guys in Bilaq! Why the hell do I like that?

Vadim let out a cloud of smoke. "Everything is learnable these days, thanks to the internet. Just go to YouTube and look at dog training videos."

Karma envied Vadim for speaking English with no trace of a foreign accent. She knew he was from a Slavic country, but his wife had mentioned it once, and she had forgotten which one. "Where are you from, by the way?"

He leaned in and scratched his chin. "Originally, from Moldova."

"Ah! You were born there?"

"Yeah."

Baladi pulled Karma forward as he eyed a squirrel in the tree in front of Vadim's house. Karma got a treat from her pants pocket and gave it to him.

"Yep, that's the way to do it. Distract him with treats when he misbehaves," Vadim said, petting Baladi on the back. Baladi wagged his tail.

Karma looked up at him, giving him a curious look. "How come you don't have an accent?"

Vadim gave a broad smile, showing his dimples. "Oh. I worked on it. I didn't want to stand out."

"I'll always stand out," she said. "I can't get rid of that damn accent."

He laughed. "You just need to practice," he said. "Besides, an accent is a sign of bravery."

"Bravery? How come?"

"When you hear an accent, you realize you're talking to an immigrant who endured a lot to make it in a foreign land. Someone who is constantly improving himself, learning, doing better."

Karma felt butterflies in her stomach. This guy is charming!

She had a sudden urge to touch him everywhere, anywhere, just to be close to him. She wanted to trace her fingertips along the contours of his face, to glide them down the firm planes of his chest, to grasp his muscled arms.

Damn it. I might just mount him right now. "Yeah, I see your point. I never thought of it this way."

He blew out some smoke that filled Karma's nostrils. "I think I read that somewhere on Instagram," he said.

They both laughed.

Their conversation was interrupted by the emergence of a young boy, about three or four years old, carrying a toy gun from the side door. He was a carbon copy of his dad—with the same reddish hair, blue eyes, round face, and big ears.

"Hey, buddy. What's up?" said Vadim, looking at his son.

The boy didn't respond; instead, he stared at both Karma and Baladi.

"This is our neighbor," he said, looking Karma up and down with a look that made her blush. "Sorry, I forgot your name," he added.

"Karma."

"Yes! Now I remember. Beautiful name. I'm Vadim, and this is my buddy, Palev."

"Hi, Palev," said Karma. "You like dogs?" she asked, leaning down to reach the boy. "This is Baladi. You can pet him."

The boy didn't move.

Vadim took the boy's hand and put it on the dog. "Come on, just try."

His hand brushed against Karma.

An image formed before her.

Vadim was sitting on a clean bathroom floor, leaning by the door where towels and bathrobes hung from hooks. Vadim's hands covered his head, and he was crying. He heaved a couple of times, then started breathing heavily as if he was having a panic attack.

The image disappeared just as quickly as it had appeared.

Karma looked at Vadim. What was the reason for his sadness? He seems happy, she thought. Committed husband and a good dad.

She felt an overwhelming urge to hug him. The hormones were messing with her head.

"Okay, I must go," she said, eager to leave before Vadim caught on to how she was feeling. "I need to make dinner; my husband will be home soon." She made sure to emphasize the word "husband."

She turned around and started heading back home, back to Jasmine Drive. As she reached the first corner, Danielle stood under an oak tree, looking somehow more mature and less angry.

"He's cute. Isn't he?" said Danielle, grinning tauntingly.

"Shut up, Danielle," said Karma, and she kept walking. Danielle walked behind her. Karma wondered if Lilith was talking to her instead of Danielle. There was something about the maturity of the voice that signaled the appearance of Lilith over Danielle.

Danielle grabbed a strand of her black hair and started twirling it around her finger. "You know this is your chance. He's perfect for you. Also, he is a foreigner, so he gets you. He's the one. This is your chance to live a little."

"I'm married, and he's married too, you idiot," said Karma.

"And you think that would stop men? What a fool you are," said Danielle. "Look at your husband. That didn't stop him."

Danielle's words stabbed Karma's heart. She wasn't over the pain of what Jamal had done or was destined to do. "Leave me alone," Karma said and kept walking. "I don't work this way. I have morals and rules that guide me in life. Not like you, where everything goes."

Danielle/Lilith sighed. "And how did these rules work out for you, ha?"

Why did this demon get such satisfaction out of taunting her? "Leave me the fuck alone," shouted Karma turning her head sideways.

As she neared her house, her phone buzzed in her pocket. She fished it out of her down jacket and looked at the screen—a text from Jamal.

Jamal: Working late. Don't wait for me. Take good care of yourself and the baby. Love you!

He's probably screwing that bitch cunt, Gina, as we speak. Fuck him and his mom, too.

A wave of nausea washed over her. She clenched her jaw and walked back to Vadim's house.

She passed by Danielle, who stood by the corner, vaping and looking at her phone. When she saw Karma, she smiled. "Now, we're talking."

"Fuck you."

Karma continued to walk. Vadim remained outside, talking with his son.

"Hey," said Karma.

"You're back," said Vadim, dimples showing.

Karma shifted her weight from one foot to the other. "I forgot to ask you. Do you know of places that hire translators? Since you speak multiple languages, I was wondering if you have any connections. Your wife mentioned you do freelance translation work. I'm looking for a job."

Vadim smiled. "Yeah, I can help for sure. What's your phone number? I can text you some contacts."

Karma gave him her phone number.

Chapter 10

IT'S HARD TO fall in love when you are in my condition. People like us are not meant to fall in love; we're meant to suffer. Falling in love is dangerous because we would have to lie to our loved ones, and eventually, we would hurt them. For people like us, it's better not to feel. For people like us, we have to numb our emotions. It's dangerous to get attached. We just need to be to exist. Feelings are out of the equation.

Karma was seated cross-legged in the middle of her bed. She sighed as she continued reading.

I know there is a dark side inside of me, and it scares me. Sometimes, I enjoy seeing those visions. I enjoy seeing the suffering. The tears. The meltdowns. I enjoy being the spectator of the macabre. I even enjoy seeing death before it happens. I enjoy watching people's eyes when their life drifts away, when their soul escapes their bodies. I enjoy seeing the evil before it occurs. The happy visions bore me, and I quickly forgot about them. They never stay with me. Seeing people enjoying life is dull and doesn't evoke any emotions in me. I want to see the blood, the gore. I want to see death.

Why was I created like this? What did my mom eat when she was pregnant with me? I know that hell awaits me when I face my own death. No one with thoughts like mine deserves to go to heaven. That's my reality, and I fully accept it. Yes, my fat neighbor Malik was right. I'm the daughter of Satan.

Karma grabbed her phone. She wanted to hear from him. She needed to hear from him.

Their initial texts were few, occurring once or twice a day. They mostly discussed translation jobs, interpretation software, and where to obtain it for the best price.

Two weeks had passed since she last saw Vadim, and she hadn't stopped thinking about him. She'd considered asking him out for coffee many times, but always stopped herself.

He's a married man. This is a dangerous territory. What if I act on my fantasies?

Eventually, she relented. She couldn't tolerate the idea of not seeing him any sooner and couldn't wait to run into him. She thought about him day and night, wondering what he was doing. Was he playing ball with his kid in the backyard? Was he pleasuring his wife?

Unable to stop herself, she texted him with shaky fingers before going to bed.

They agreed to meet the next day at a coffee shop in the strip mall down the street. They settled at a table at the far end of the place. At first, they talked about translation services, then the conversation drifted toward their childhood, life in the US, and making it day by day.

"I didn't want to come here," he admitted, hands wrapped around the coffee cup. "My wife dragged me."

It wasn't a good sign that he was bringing up his wife. "Really? Where did you meet?"

He took a sip from his coffee. "We met in India. She was there on vacation, and I was there with my uncle, trying to set up a business. His business ultimately went bust," he frowned. "We met on the beach in Goa."

"Sounds romantic," she said, smiling and tilting her head.

He looked up at Karma, eyes smoldering. "Yeah. It was."

"Was?"

He smiled sadly. "Well, it still is. Anyway. We stayed in India for a month, then she brought me here with her, and the rest is history."

She imagined them in bed after making love, her selling him the idea of moving to the US, her head on his bare chest. "Why don't you like it here?"

He sighed. "Well, the culture, mostly. Here, people work for retirement, and then they're too old and sick to travel. What a life wasted! You should not wait until you're seventy to enjoy life, to take a cruise while using a walker."

Karma let out a quiet laugh. "Yeah. I hear ya." She twirled the rim of her coffee cup with her finger.

"So, are you happy here?" he asked, leaning back against the chair.

A gulf opened in Karma's stomach. She had been raised to put her happiness last, behind her parents, behind her husband, even a cheating husband. "I don't know. I like the neighborhood and my dog." She sighed. "I just feel lonely here, sometimes."

"What about your husband? You didn't mention him?"

Karma's cheeks flushed. "He's a surgeon. He's always working. I hardly see him."

"Must be tough."

"It is," she said in a quiet voice, almost whispering.

Vadim moved his coffee cup aside so that the back of his hand was close to the back of hers, almost close enough to touch, but not quite. The tingle between her legs turned into a tremor.

"If you were my wife, I'd find a way to work less and spend more time at home," he said with a glint in his eyes.

She felt her heart jump out of her chest, and for a minute, she had a hard time breathing. Is he flirting? It must be. This isn't just friendly talk.

FROM THERE, THEIR texting ascended to a higher level.

Vadim: If I were your husband, I'd hold you in my arms every chance I could get.

She immediately changed the passcode on her phone and then logged into iCloud, ensuring that her texts were not backed up there. She didn't need more drama in her life.

She spent most days texting back and forth with Vadim, sometimes about work and sometimes about how he could be a better husband.

Vadim sent her some articles about dog training techniques, followed by some memes about life in the US. She smiled and sent him links to some TikTok videos she came across.

All day, she felt elated, like a teenager who had just met her first crush.

Her crushes in Bilaq had been few and far between, and she mostly kept her feelings to herself. She would not dare to share her illicit thoughts with anyone, especially her mom. She would observe boys from afar and wonder if she would end up with a good, handsome husband someday.

Vadim opened up something in her, something she hadn't felt in a very long time. Not even when she first met Jamal. That feeling of her heart beating so fast in excitement, as if she was having a heart attack, the butterflies in her stomach, the sense of floating in the air. Vadim blasted that door wide open, and she was not ready to close it yet. She wanted more of his texts. She wanted more of him. She wanted to see him.

That night, when Jamal came home, she was already in bed, reading a novel.

"Let me get in the shower quickly. I don't want to give you any of the hospital germs."

Karma gave him a forced smile and then went back to her book. She heard the water running in the shower in their master bedroom, and suddenly, the idea of Jamal being on top of her repulsed her. She got her phone from its charger on the bedside table and started scrolling through her Instagram feed. She felt a ping of jealousy as she saw a picture of some of her friends from Bilaq lounging around a pool at a fancy hotel by the Red Sea.

She opened the messages app and looked at Vadim's previous messages. Was he making love to his wife right now? Was he stroking her blonde, silky hair? Was he looking deep into her blue eyes? Was he running his hands all over her pale, soft skin?

She wondered why he would trade his wife for her. A Middle Eastern woman with dark features that might put him off.

In Bilaq, parents were thrilled if their daughter was born beida, with fair skin. Karma was definitely not beautiful, but she was not ugly. She knew that many guys, including Jamal, found her attractive.

Does Vadim find me attractive?

She needed to see him. Their connection was special. He had to feel it, too.

Karma: Hey. Are you awake?

She immediately regretted the late-night message. But two seconds later...

Vadim: Yep. I always stay up late.

She smiled.

Karma: I'm having trouble with the translation software you recommended. Some of its features are locked, and I'm unsure how to unlock them. Are you around tomorrow?

She didn't want to make it about work, but if Jamal came out of the shower or if Vadim's wife was looking over his shoulder, at least this would be a legitimate reason for a late-night message.

Vadim: Yeah. Wanna bring your laptop to the library tomorrow? Maybe at 4:00 PM?

Not the library! Where his wife works!

Karma: 4:00 works, but can we meet at the coffee place instead? I need my Java :)

Karma pinned a mental note to order a decaf coffee without him noticing. According to all the books she had read, caffeine and pregnancy should not mix.

Vadim: Yes! I'm looking forward to seeing you.

She felt her fingers tremble as she typed out a goodbye. He was looking forward to it. Her heart rate elevated.

"Who are you texting so late?" Jamal asked, having just emerged from the shower with a white towel wrapped around his waist.

A lump lodged in her throat. "Uh, just an old friend from Bilaq. She's having trouble sleeping. Marriage issues, and I'm trying to help."

Jamal took off the towel, threw it on the bed, and stood naked in front of her, ready for her. "I had a very stressful day," said Jamal as he climbed on top of her.

A wave of nausea overcame her, and she jumped out of bed and went to vomit up her dinner.

SHE COULD HARDLY focus on anything but her date with Vadim. She stayed in bed until Jamal left for work or whatever the hell he was going to do, then opened her wardrobe in search of the perfect outfit.

Could he tell she was pregnant? No, how could he, unless he was a mind-reader? Though stranger things had been happening lately. But she was not showing yet and had actually lost weight during her first trimester.

She scanned her closet for something elegant and sexy. But also appropriate for a coffee shop. She settled on a beige tunic that accentuated her breasts and paired it with black leggings and brown leather boots. She walked Baladi once and watched some mindless TV, anxiously waiting for her rendezvous.

At 4:00 sharp, she was outside the coffee shop. She could hear the hum of the conversations and the soft clinking of cups. He showed up at 4:03. As soon as she saw him, her heart skipped a beat, and she felt her cheeks burn. She tried to open her mouth to say hi, but she couldn't utter a word, paralyzed by fear and excitement. She waved her hand.

He ran a hand through his hair, a sheepish smile spreading across his face. "Sorry, I'm a bit late. Palev threw a tantrum right before coming here. Good thing Amanda was home."

Amanda. What a buzz kill.

She led the way to their usual table at the far end of the place, a secluded spot that felt like a small sanctuary away from the chaos of the coffee shop. The aroma of freshly ground coffee beans and baked goods filled the air.

She insisted on paying for the coffee, saying she owed him for all his help with the translation. She navigated to the counter, where the barista greeted her with a familiar smile. She ordered their coffees, sneaking in a decaf for herself. Back at their table, surrounded by the occasional hiss of the espresso machine, she felt the bubble of their shared space grow more intimate.

Karma pulled her computer out of her big brown satchel and showed him the issues she was facing with the software. He showed her a couple of tricks. Their hands brushed briefly, and she felt him squeeze her index finger.

Did I imagine that?

She ignored what he was showing her on the computer. Instead, she stared deeply into his blue eyes and imagined caressing his neatly trimmed red beard.

"Get it now?" he asked, breaking her trance.

Oh, to kiss those lips. "Yeah, yeah, thanks. I guess I should get home." Gazing out the window, she saw it was already dark.

"Would you like me to walk you back home?" he offered, his voice cutting through the crisp evening.

She nodded.

They walked for a few minutes when she suddenly stopped by the side of the road and faced a split-level house with faded siding where an old cat lady lived.

He looked puzzled. "Is everything okay?"

She quickly scanned the old lady's yard, filled with cat statues and chimes, then looked at him—really looked at him, her eyes reflecting under the glow of a nearby street lamp.

"What is it?" he asked, crossing his eyebrows.

"I must kiss you," she said, registering the look of shock on his face and feeling a moment of regret and rejection.

But then he looked around, grabbed her hand, and tugged her to the side of the old lady's house. Luckily, no vision slowed her down from what she hoped would happen next. They took a dirt path that ran alongside the side of the house to a small, undeveloped, woodsy area tucked between houses. She walked silently with him, her heart pounding in her ears.

He stopped by an old oak tree and looked at her. "You're shivering," he said.

She hadn't even noticed. "I am. I don't do things like this. I'm a good girl," she whispered, the words spilling out.

He pulled her into a long hug. He smelled of aftershave and cigarettes, a contrast to the earthy scents surrounding them. She held him tightly, then let go.

"Better?" he asked, looking deep into her eyes.

"Yes," she whispered.

She took a few steps back, then leaned against the tree trunk. Knowing it was rarely frequented, especially at this time of year, she confidently set her satchel on the leaf-covered ground.

He rested his arm on the tree, tilted his head, and kissed her.

Fireworks exploded inside and outside. Her heart melted. Her insides melted, and she felt a wetness between her legs. When he let go, she put her hands on his face and touched his beard, just as she had dreamed.

"You're so sexy," she said.

He smiled.

She kissed him, feeling the taste of his tongue. "I want more," she whispered.

"I can't," he said, sounding sad.

"Please," she begged, the need to have him burning inside of her.

"Karma, don't do this to me. You're so sexy, smart, and beautiful. I just can't."

She placed her hand on his crotch and felt his manhood. "You're ready," she said.

He looked at her, torn. "Oh, yeah, but..."

She kissed him again.

He grabbed her shoulders, twirled her around, and pressed her against the tree, her face resting on her forearm, which was resting on the trunk. He unzipped his fly, unleashing butterflies in her belly. He kissed her neck while he lowered her leggings. He ran his fingers on her thighs, then pulled down her underwear.

She could hear his heavy breathing.

He entered her as he twisted her nipple with one hand while the other hand rested on the tree. She knew there was no way back. It was done.

Her moans were loud.

"Shh," he said, placing one hand on her mouth. She felt herself choking, but that feeling excited her, giving her an immense wave of pleasure on the verge of climaxing, but she held on. She wanted to be with him when the moment came.

He kept pounding on her as she faced the tree. Fast, then slow, then repeating. She felt him shudder as he released a faint moan. With her eyes closed, she came, and for the first time, she felt something different, something she had not felt before.

A baby's kick.

He was alive.

She smiled between her multiple orgasms as she devoured the waves of her pleasure. One wave after the other, after the other. She waited a bit, then turned around to face him. His face was flushed.

They locked eyes. He had tears in his eyes.

He walked her back home in silence. She knew—whatever had happened in those woods, the old Karma was dead. She had crossed so many boundaries, so many rules and limitations. Shedding her old self, she suddenly felt new. She was finally living.

Karma couldn't stop thinking about the baby's kick. "How did I feel it so early in my pregnancy?" she wondered. According to all the books she had read, wasn't she supposed to feel it later? Maybe it was time to trash all those books. She wasn't normal; her pregnancy wasn't normal. The only good thing that would come from her messed-up situation was her baby.

"Please, God, take good care of my child," she prayed silently, resting a hand gently on her belly. She beamed as she felt another kick.

Chapter 11

K ARMA COULDN'T BELIEVE she had done the unthinkable. She, the woman from Bilaq, who had never even kissed a man before she got married, had cheated on her husband with a married man in a public place in the middle of the suburbs. How could she have done that? What kind of curse had demonic Danielle cast on her, forcing her to stray in this horrendous manner?

What surprised Karma most was that... she was happy. She felt a rebirth, a resurrection. Karma was finding it hard to recognize the new her. What happened to the shy, good-girl Karma? Could someone change that quickly without an external interface, without a supernatural influence?

Damn you, Danielle.

Karma didn't hear from Vadim that night, or the day after, or the day after. She started to get antsy. She wanted more of him, more of his body, more of that life. She wanted more of that orgasm. That intense feeling of pleasure she had never experienced with Jamal before. Her orgasms with Jamal, if you even called them that, were small, insignificant, short, and hardly noticeable. She had no clue. She thought that was it, and that was what sex was all about. She had no idea there was more. So much more.

What is going on with Vadim? Does he feel guilty? Maybe I'm not really good with this whole sex thing, and his wife is way better.

Jamal was her only sexual experience, and he was the one who made all the moves. What she had done with Vadim was a first. She'd initiated it.

Did his wife find out?

She was tempted to text him, call him, or walk by his house, but she held back because she didn't want to appear needy or pushy.

On the third day after their lovemaking in the woods, she got a text from him.

Vadim: Hey. Just checking on the translation gigs. How is it going?

What? No mention of that night? Is his wife poking around?

Karma: Yeah. Plugging along. Translation is not for the faint of heart.

She wouldn't mention that night in case his wife was monitoring their conversations.

Vadim: I hear ya. Let me know if you need anything. Always up for helping my neighbor.

Neighbor? Is that a code?

Karma: Can you meet up to go through some translation "stuff"?

She made sure to put quotes around the word stuff. Hopefully, he would get the message.

Vadim: I'm free at 8:00 tonight. Or is that too late?

Little explosions detonated all her nerve endings. He wanted to see her. Tonight.

Karma: Works for me. Husband is working late.

She made it a point to refer to Jamal as her husband. Somehow, typing or uttering his name made him real, made her actions more sinister, and made her even more despicable.

Vadim: Okay. See you at the coffee place?

Karma: Yep. Same place! Same table.

When she started walking to the meeting place, her heart was racing so fast; she felt she would just have a heart attack and drop dead in the middle of the street. Flashbacks from that night played before her, his moans, the feel of him pumping inside her.

She got there on time, but instead of seeing him, Danielle was waiting by the entrance.

"You?" said Karma, shaking her head. "What the hell are you doing here?"

She tilted her head with a smile. "Grabbing some coffee. Isn't that what you're doing too?"

"Leave me alone, bitch." Karma couldn't believe her ears. How could she say this vulgar word to someone out in public?

"Karma, Karma. Listen, you started all of this. You piqued my interest when you began following me. You figured me out very quickly. No one else has done that but you. We're connected. Don't you see? We're like the yin and yang. We're different, but we can never be separated."

Karma stepped back.. "Stay away from me."

"You're mine now," Danielle whispered. "And I always collect."

Karma stopped listening and turned her head as she saw Vadim approaching the store.

"Looks like lover boy is here," said Danielle, smiling. "I'll leave you two to your shenanigans. I just came here to say... you're doing well."

"I'm sorry I'm late," said Vadim, gasping for air. "Just some drama at home."

"Is everything okay?" Karma asked.

"Yeah. Don't worry about it. I took care of it."

When Karma turned her head to check on Danielle, she was already gone. She doubted Vadim had even noticed her existence in the first place.

Karma and Vadim didn't even bother to go inside the coffee shop. They walked directly to the woods, to the same tree, the only witness to their copulation.

Their lovemaking was fierce, and this time, she didn't have to ask for it. When she let out her shouts of pleasure, he covered her mouth with his hand and watched her intently as one wave after the other ran through her veins. He wrapped his hand around her neck, augmenting her pleasure, making her want more, more of him. She didn't want him to stop. Ever.

When he walked her back home, he stopped and said, "We shouldn't do this again." He sighed, tears welling in his eyes. "I love my family. I don't ever want to leave them."

Karma raised her eyebrows. "Who's asking you to leave them?"

His gaze dropped to the ground. "Well, what's the end game here?" he asked.

"There is no end game. Let's just take it one day at a time."

She couldn't believe she was saying these words to a married man. Take it one day at a time. Where did she hear that? From Dr. Phil?

❋ ❋ ❋

KARMA AND VADIM met at least three times a week at the same spot. The woods became a constant reminder of her affair, and the mere sight of them as she walked the dog excited her to no end, making her heart pound and causing a stir between her legs.

One day, as Karma walked back home after spending some time with Vadim, she encountered Danielle standing by the corner with a vape in her mouth. "You are glowing," Danielle said.

"You? Again," said Karma, shaking her head. "Aren't you young to be smoking?" How old is this demon really?

"All that sex is doing you some good," Danielle said, ignoring her comment.

"Leave me alone."

She blew out a puff of smoke. "Your son is lucky. He will have two fathers," she said.

Karma clutched her belly. "What the hell are you talking about? You know his dad is Jamal." For better or for worse.

She snickered. "Really? Haven't you heard of the Bari Indians?"

Karma shook her head. "The who?"

Danielle inhaled. "The Bari Indians. They are an indigenous people in Colombia."

"And? Why should I care?"

"You should. They believe that multiple men can impregnate a woman with one child and that having two fathers is better than having one. Learn from their wisdom. Two fathers are better than one."

The baby kicked.

Karma put her hand on her belly, trying to make sure she hadn't imagined the baby's movement. "Seriously? Do you believe that bullshit? How do you even know this stuff? You never struck me as a reader."

Danielle smiled. "There is a lot you don't know about me. Don't be surprised if your child has dimples or even more."

During those days of her extramarital adventure, Karma had never been happier or more productive. She spent her days tidying up, making dinner, walking Baladi, and waiting to see Vadim. They'd text most of the day, and by the time they saw each other, they wouldn't say much. They'd lose themselves to their lovemaking, to the pleasure of the intertwining of their bodies. She tried to avoid Jamal as much as she could. She didn't want to deal with her whirlwind of contradictory emotions, guilt, and the need for revenge, to show that bastard that screwing the neighbor was never something she'd agree to, even if he thought she was a submissive wife who would go along with anything her husband wanted or desired.

"You look different these days," Jamal told her one evening while they had dinner. "This pregnancy is really agreeing with you now."

Afraid to look him in the eyes, she focused her attention on the rice and lentil dish she was trying to eat. She could feel the intense beating of her heart in her throat.

He smiled, tilting his head. "You look healthier, happier somehow. This baby is good for you."

She moved the lentils with her fork, avoiding any eye contact. She could hear the faint sound of a lawn mower.

"I do feel better. You know, the second trimester is supposed to be the best." She bit her lower lip. "Also, the baby is kicking, and that makes me happy. He's healthy."

Jamal leaned back in his chair. "I keep missing his kicks. I want to feel them."

She lifted her head and finally looked him in the eye. "Well, you're never around."

He put his fork down on his plate, almost banging it. "What's that supposed to mean?"

She clenched her jaw as she felt the food rising in her throat. Was he going to throw that fork at her? She pushed her plate away and pushed her chair back to put some distance between them. "Can we please not fight? I'm sorry. Okay? Can we drop it? I appreciate everything you do for this family."

"Fine," said Jamal, then took a sip of water. "Our ultrasound is tomorrow, isn't it?"

"Yeah, it's a boy," she said, massaging her abdomen.

"Really? What makes you sure it's a boy?"

"Just a hunch. The mother always knows." She looked at him and forced a smile. She kind of hoped Danielle was wrong; it would mean she really was full of shit and just tormenting Karma with all the demonic talk.

Jamal smiled. "I'm sorry I snapped. I'm just exhausted." He placed his arm on the table, then reached for her hand. "All that work at the hospital is wearing me down. You're right. I need to cut down my hours, so I have time to be around you and the baby."

That or your affair with Gina!

He stood up from his chair and kissed her forehead. "I'm sorry. Please forgive me," he said.

From the outside, they appeared to be the perfect couple, enjoying a nice meal. What a facade. They were both cheaters living in a house of cards bound to crumble down at any minute.

"Hello, you there? You got quiet on me," he said, waving his hand in front of her face.

She shook her head as if trying to snap back to the present. "Yeah, I'm here. Sorry. Just a brain fog."

Later, as she was putting on her nightgown, Jamal was already waiting for her in bed, making it clear that he wanted her. She obliged, not wanting him to suspect anything or unleash his wrath, for she didn't want him to discover that her desires were being met elsewhere. So, she closed her eyes and imagined Vadim instead.

When he finished, he traced circles around her belly with his hand. He then put his ear to it. "Come on, baby, kick for me. Come on. Don't do it just for Mommy."

Karma smiled. "Maybe he likes me more."

"You keep referring to the baby as he. You seem so sure of that mother hunch."

"Well, I am."

"We'll find out tomorrow!" he said, sitting up, leaning against the bed frame, and pulling the down comforter over himself.

Karma hated it when he slept naked, especially after their lovemaking. She wished he would shower and put on some pants or something.

"You know, I think you are starting to show," he said, looking at her. "Don't you think we should announce our news? Have you told your friends yet?"

She shook her head. "Not yet. I'm barely showing anyway."

He shrugged. "I think we're ready. Let's share our good news with the world. Just post an announcement on Facebook or Instagram or one of those social media channels you're always on."

Karma looked down at her belly. Had Vadim noticed? "I'm not ready yet to announce."

"Why not?"

She bit the edge of her lip. "I don't know. I guess I'm superstitious. You know. El Ein?"

A laugh escaped his lips. "El Ein? The Evil Eye. Seriously? Come on, babe, don't listen to your mom."

Her posture stiffened. "It's not about my mom. I really believe people, especially those who are jealous of you, can jinx your good fortune."

He chuckled softly. "Maybe you should get rid of some of those toxic people in your life. Who needs this drama?"

She nodded slowly. "Yeah, you're right. There are a lot of people I would need to unfollow."

Jamal was suddenly in a good mood, and it bothered her. She didn't want him to be a loving husband because this would make her feel guilty, even though she felt no remorse. Thinking of him as the horrible cheating husband justified her own cheating.

She couldn't sleep that night and kept thinking of the fact that she'd started to show. Vadim had never seen her naked since all of their lovemaking happened in the dark, in the woods, with her mostly dressed. Did he ever put his hands on my belly while inside me?

What would he do when he found out she was pregnant? Would he end things?

The idea of not having Vadim in her life terrified her. She needed him

After tossing and turning for hours, she slipped out of bed. Jamal had said he'd be working late, finishing patient reports. As she padded past his office, she saw the faint glow of his laptop under the door. She pushed it open slightly. He was hunched over his desk, typing quickly. "Still working?" she asked softly.

"Yeah. I'm behind on some cases," he said without turning.

"Patient reports again?"

"Mhm." He finally turned to look at her, but not directly, his eyes hovered over her shoulder

She stood silently, trying to read his expression. Her chest tightened. "Okay. Goodnight," she whispered. As she walked back to their bedroom, her pulse quickened. He is probably chatting with that bitch!

❋ ❋ ❋

THE NEXT MORNING, she and Jamal headed to the doctor's for a routine checkup and to find out the baby's sex.

"I already know," she said in the car, staring out the window. She was shivering and hugging herself. Jamal didn't even notice and didn't offer to turn up the heat.

"Yeah, yeah, mother's hunch and all that," he said, his eyes on the road.

She turned around and faced him. "Wanna bet?"

"Sure," he said, smiling.

"If I win, I want to go on a vacation with my girlfriends for the weekend." She had already practiced that line multiple times in her head.

He crossed his eyebrows. "What girlfriends?"

Oh, she didn't think about the names. So stupid. She had to think fast.

"Jill and Kathy," she blurted, hoping she hadn't ruined her chance to have two full days with Vadim.

"Ha? Remind me again, who are these people?" He turned his head towards her.

"Our neighbors. Come on. You know, Jill, of course. And Kathy lives by the high school," she said, avoiding eye contact in hopes he wouldn't detect the lie.

"Ah, yeah. Sorry, a lot on my mind, and I can't keep up with your friends. Anyway, it's a deal. If we're having a boy, you'll get your girlfriends' weekend," he said, tapping on the steering wheel as if he were sealing the deal. "And if it's a girl, well, I get what I like. You know that." He winked.

She knew what he wanted. Isn't Gina giving him that? Pleasuring him orally?

After waiting for more than 30 minutes, during which Karma and Jamal didn't exchange a word, Karma sat on the edge of the examination table. The doctor finally arrived, sporting a big smile on his face.

"Are you ready to know the gender?" Dr. Grahm, a chubby middle-aged man with round glasses and gray hair, asked. He looked at the ultrasound and then looked at Jamal and Karma.

Karma was sitting up on a hospital bed with a white sheet covering her legs. Dr. Grahm had the wand of the ultrasound machine placed on her belly.

"Yes," said Jamal, smiling while Karma remained silent. She felt some shivers from the cold gel that Dr. Grahm placed around her belly.

What if the baby had two fathers, like Danielle had told her? What if he had three legs and three arms? What if Dr. Graham exposes her cheating to her husband?

Stop it, Karma. Stop it. You're going insane.

❀ ❀ ❀

ON THE WAY back, Jamal was in seventh heaven. "I can't believe we are having a boy. You were right. You were absolutely right. Let's go out and celebrate. Whatever you want. Italian. Chinese. Indian? No. Indian might be too spicy for you. Let's go for Italian."

Karma was not even listening. Her mind was focused on one thing—Vadim. "Does that mean I get my girls' weekend?" she asked.

"Ha! Girls' weekend? Yeah. Yeah. Sure. Sure. Just make sure to go soon. We don't want any risks to happen to the baby while you're away from me." He turned his head toward her and placed his hand on her belly. "Just pick a place within two hours from home."

Karma planned the romantic escape, just the two of them, away from Vadim's wife and his son, away from Jamal and Baladi, away from crazy Danielle and all the idiots in the neighborhood. She fantasized about the two of them in a cabin in the mountains, making love by the fireplace. She was aware that she had to tell him that she was pregnant, that soon enough, she wouldn't be able to see him, and that making love in the woods while she was in her third trimester wasn't the smartest of ideas.

Between the hours of three and four in the morning, and after she had finished scrolling her Instagram and TikTok feeds, and as Jamal was snoring right beside her, his naked body against her thigh, she finally made up her mind. After their getaway, she was going to end it. As much as it would pain her to do so, she had no choice but to focus on the next chapter of her life: the baby. She quietly lifted the edge of her side of the mattress, trying not to disturb Jamal, and pulled out the journal.

I can't stop thinking about sex. I see it everywhere. I imagine it in my dreams. I want to have it so badly, but how? I don't see myself getting married anytime soon, and that's the only legitimate way for women here to have sex, unlike men who can just drive to the next town and sleep with foreign prostitutes. Why am I like this? Women are not supposed to think constantly about sex like men. We are supposed to hate sex. We just have to be ready for our husbands when the urge strikes, but I'm not like that. Not at all. I always feel something stirring between my legs, and I'm always wet down there. I recently discovered the pleasure of touching myself, and I just can't stop doing it. I rub and rub until I feel it coming, until I get transferred to heaven and back, until my insides scream from pleasure.

Why am I like this? Is this also part of my condition? Is this even fixable? Sometimes I pray to God to end my life. I can't live with myself. Knowing that I'm vile. Dirty. Evil. A disgusting creature who can't stop herself from doing the unthinkable. What's the point of my existence, really? Why did God create me to suffer like this?

Karma shook her head and threw the journal on the bed. This woman needs to get a life. It has to be Danielle who sent me this. It has her fingerprints all over it. She wants to mess with my head.

Chapter 12

Now that she'd convinced Jamal that she had to go away for the weekend, she needed to work on Vadim. Would he agree to leave his family for the weekend and be with her? Would he be able to convince his wife? She waited a couple of days before making any contact with him, wanting him to miss her and to spend more time with her.

Karma: Same

She finally texted him when she couldn't stand to be apart for another minute. "Same" was the code they had agreed on when they wanted to meet at the coffee place at 8:00 PM.

When she met him outside the store, he was finishing a cigarette. As soon as he saw her, he threw the cigarette butt on the sidewalk and smiled. He tilted his head to the side, which she took as his way of asking her to go to the woods.

"Let's go inside," she said.

"Oh? Is everything all right?" he asked, a look of disappointment on his face.

"Yeah, I need to talk."

"Oh, no. I hate it when women say that. What's going on?" he said, running his fingers through his reddish beard.

"Everything is okay. Trust me. Just come inside," she said, taking his hand and pulling him inside the store. That was a bold move on her part. Somehow, she didn't care if they got caught.

When she told him what she had in mind—a romantic getaway in the mountains—he hesitated.

"Baby, this sounds amazing, but what will I tell Amanda, especially since we're leaving her alone with Palev?" He rubbed his hand on his face. He opened his mouth but closed it again. "I don't know, baby. I don't know. I don't think I can pull it off."

"Can you say that you're going to visit a friend?" she said in a gentle tone, then took a sip from her hot latte.

He jiggled his leg up and down. "Hmmm . . . Most of my friends are in Moldova. I really don't have friends here."

"Okay, let me think." She ran her finger around the rim of her plastic cup of coffee. "What about a family emergency? Do you have any relatives in the States?"

He shook his head. "Nope. All in Moldova."

"I see," she said, tucking a strand of her wavy brown hair behind her ear and focusing her attention on his leg, which was still bouncing. "What about a work trip?"

He arched an eyebrow, leaning forward slightly. "What kind of a work trip?"

She leaned in, too, her eyes sparkling. "Maybe you could say that you were asked to interpret for the State Department, like a group of Russian students on a tour sponsored by the US government, who need interpreters."

He smiled. "Ha! That's a good one." He leaned back in his chair. "How did you come up with it?"

She laughed. "I don't know. I have a wild imagination."

Lying and deceiving were so natural now.

They both headed home that day without making love. She wanted him to ache for her, to enjoy her even more, and to save all his desires and energy for their weekend alone.

Karma took care of the reservations, booking a private cabin in the mountains with a fireplace, a hot tub, easy access to the woodsy trails, and floor-to-ceiling windows that showcased the rustic view. She picked a place that would come as close as possible to the lovers' cabins that she had read about in many of the romance novels she devoured.

It had to be perfect. It would be their last time together.

She paid with her debit card, using some of her savings that Jamal had no access to, money her parents had given to her as a wedding present. Right after she paid, she felt dirty, like a cheap whore. *I used my parents' hard-earned money on sluttish activities, but you know what? Jamal started this whole mess. What I'm doing is self-care.*

In the days leading up to the getaway, she couldn't focus on anything, not even Baladi. She kept imagining scenes in her head of what they would do there and what she would tell him. She stayed in bed, mostly scrolling through social media for distraction. She avoided eye contact with Jamal, as she had enough on her plate.

They agreed to leave on Saturday morning and return Sunday evening, a short and sweet arrangement. She asked Jamal to drop her off at Jill's house, although Jill was still in rehab, and Jamal was unaware of her location. When the coast was clear, she walked a few blocks down the street to meet Vadim in the parking lot of their neighborhood church, which was surrounded by pine trees, shielding them from the curious eyes of neighbors.

Everything worked according to plan. In his black SUV, on the way to the cabin, they listened to music and talked about their childhood.

He told her he lost his virginity when he was fourteen.

She raised her eyebrows. "Seriously? That young. I didn't even know where babies came from at that age!"

He laughed.

"Did it mess with your head?" she asked, fiddling with the radio to change the channel.

"What?"

"I mean, having sex with girls that early? Did it, like, fuck you up?" she said as she settled on a station playing sixties rock.

He chuckled. "Are you kidding me? Of course not. I felt great. Manly. I couldn't stop thinking about sex. I still can't, actually."

"Yeah, I can see that."

They both laughed.

She told him that Jamal was her first.

"Really? You mean you were a virgin when you got married? I never pegged you to be that type. You know. With us. You sort of started things." He smiled slyly.

"Well, people change," she said, then grew quiet as she pondered the weight of these words.

"How is Jamal as a lover?" he asked.

She raised her eyebrows. "Seriously? You wanna know that? Why?"

"I don't know. Just curious, I guess." He turned his head toward her. "Do you enjoy having sex with him?"

She saw a look of mischief on his face. She let out a long sigh. "I don't want to discuss Jamal. Not now. Don't ruin the mood. All I can tell you is you're a better lover."

He smiled. "Of course I am." He stretched his arm and ran his fingers along her thigh. He slid his fingers underneath her blue dress and started rubbing her wetness.

"And very humble, too," she said between moans.

They laughed again.

He let out a cry of pleasure. "You're always ready for me, aren't you, my sexy Arab princess?"

Arab princess, his new pet name for her. She was not sure how she felt about it.

When they got to the cabin, Karma was pleased to see that it looked very similar to the pictures she'd seen online. The rustic furniture smelled of pine wood, and the creaky hardwood floors added to the charm. A bathtub was positioned in front of the fireplace, and a vintage-style bed with a wooden frame stood nearby. Large windows overlooked the mountains, and rocking chairs were on the front porch.

When they put their stuff down, they moved to the bedroom.

"Gorgeous. Isn't it?" said Karma, running her hand along the bed's wooden frame. "Especially that bathtub right in the middle."

Vadim didn't respond and hardly looked around the room. Instead, he grabbed Karma's arm, kissed her, then ran his hand on her breast. When she felt his erection against her crotch, she stopped him.

"Let's go explore the mountains first."

"What mountains? Come on," he said. "I'm ready." He grabbed her hand and placed it on his manhood.

She pulled her hand back. "I really want to take a look around first. You can wait. I want you to want me so badly." She winked.

"It'll be quick. Think of it as an appetizer before the meal. I can't go like this," he said, pointing to his visible erection.

"Please, let's go outside first."

"You're killing me. Fine, then I need to take care of this situation now since you are not going to help me." He scanned the room, then headed to the bathroom near the fireplace and closed the wooden door behind him.

Karma felt bad. *Is he doing what I think he is doing?*

She really wanted to feel him inside her, but she had to wait. She did not wish Vadim to see her naked during the day when there was a lot of sunlight. She was starting to show, and he would easily find out she was pregnant. She wanted to save the news until right before they would head back home. She wanted them to have a good time before she broke the news to him that, as much as it saddened her and as much as it broke her heart, she had no choice but to stop seeing him.

When they got out of the cabin and felt the cold, crisp air on their faces, Karma stopped and turned around.

"What is it? Did you forget something?" asked Vadim.

"No."

She pulled out her phone, snapped a picture of the cabin, and sent it as a text to Jamal:

Karma: Great cabin. The girls and I are excited. About to go hiking!

Lying had become so easy for her. It was a slippery slope. Once she started, she couldn't stop. The lie just grew bigger and bigger, snowballing out of control, and there was no way to stop it.

When they started walking up the trail, the air was cold and dry, and Vadim kept complaining that he was freezing. "I can't feel my balls," he said.

She nudged him gently with her elbow. "Come on, Vadim. You should be used to this. Remember, I'm the one from the desert."

He slowed down a bit, looking back in the direction they had come from. "Don't you think it would have been better if we were in the cabin, cuddling by the fireplace?"

"Let's enjoy this beautiful spot. We'll make love soon, promise."

He grunted.

She stopped when she noticed a couple of women walking behind them on the trail, bundled up in heavy coats and winter hats.

"Glad to see we are not the only crazy people hiking in this cold," said Vadim.

Karma ignored his comment, saying hi to the two women as they passed by. As soon as they walked in front of her, she pulled out her phone and took a picture of their backs.

"Why are you taking a picture of random strangers?" asked Vadim, shaking his head.

"You'll see."

He looked down at her phone and saw her send the picture in a text to Jamal:

Karma: Out hiking with the girls. See how far ahead of me Jill and Kathy are? I'm trying to catch up.

"Oh man, you're good. Such a good liar," said Vadim.

"I am," said Karma, then grew quiet.

Jamal: Have fun, babe, and take care. I miss you.

Vadim and Karma hiked for around two miles, but when they turned around to head back to the cabin, they realized they were lost. They found themselves surrounded by tall pine trees with no exit in sight.

Vadim snapped, "I told you I didn't want to go on this stupid hike."

Frowning, Karma crossed her arms. "Don't talk to me this way. I just wanted us to enjoy the place and not spend all of our time indoors." She battled the urge to punch him. Why is he being such a dick?

Vadim sighed, running a hand through his hair. "I left my family precisely so I could be with you indoors."

Anger built up in Karma. "I see. Do you regret it now?"

Vadim shook his head, his voice softening. "I didn't say that."

She raised her voice slightly. "You know. I left my husband, too, to be with you."

A heavy silence hung between them, punctuated only by the sounds of the forest. They eventually found their way back to the cabin with the help of a lone hiker who recognized the path. With a silent nod of gratitude, they followed the hiker's directions.

They arrived at the cabin well after sunset, the mood considerably dampened.

"Nice guy," said Vadim as they settled inside. "We could have been lost for days without him. You kept venturing off the path, and you drove me crazy."

Vadim tried to smooth things over. He lit the fire and invited her to join him in the bathtub. She asked him to dim the lights, then removed her clothes and jumped in.

He kissed her passionately on the mouth.

"I'm really sorry I was such a jerk," he said, caressing her face. "I just wanted you so badly. It was my dick speaking, not me."

She fell quiet, and suddenly, tears began to flow from her.

What the hell was she doing here? In a hot tub, naked and pregnant, with a man who wasn't her husband.

"Oh, Karma. What's the matter? Come on. I'm really sorry. I'll be good. I promise." He wiped her tears with his index finger.

"I'm okay. Just a bit emotional," she said.

He got close to her and hugged her. Her almost round belly touched his skin.

He put his hand on her stomach. "I love my women to be well-rounded."

Her heart skipped a beat. Has he found out?

Seeing the look on her face, he said, "I'm joking. You're gorgeous. I don't like skinny women. You're perfect."

They stayed in the hot tub quietly for ten minutes, watching the fireplace. Then, they got out, dried themselves with lavender-scented towels provided by the owner, and headed to bed.

She could hear her heartbeat in her ears.

He is going to find out the minute he gets on top of me.

"Can we please not do this tonight? I'm exhausted. And I can't focus," she said, moving his arm away from her.

He shifted closer to her. "What? Come on. I'm dying here. I even went on that stupid hike for you."

She turned her body away from him. "I really can't. I'm going to fall asleep."

He smiled. "I can still pleasure you while you are asleep," he put his hand between her legs.

She quickly removed his hand. "Please. I can't."

He sighed. "Okay, then, we are not leaving the cabin tomorrow. No hikes, nothing. Just sweet loving until we get back home."

He fell asleep after tossing and turning a few times while Karma stayed awake, thinking of how she would break the news to him the next day. The baby kicked most of the night while she rubbed her belly, wondering why this fetus was so active earlier than in most normal pregnancies and whether she should worry about it or take it as a sign of good health.

The next morning, he woke up and kissed her. He slid next to her, and she could feel his hardness rubbing her thigh.

"I need to tell you something," she said between kisses.

"Shh, I need to get laid first," he said, placing a hand on her breast. "My brain functions better after that."

She ran the back of her hand along his jawline. "Listen. I'm serious," she said, her eyes locked onto his.

"Okay, okay, lay it on me. Make it quick. I'm going to explode," he said, giving her half a smile.

"Vadim, I don't think we should see each other anymore," she said softly. The words hung heavy in the air.

He sat up in bed. "What? Why? Are you still mad about the hike? I told you I was sorry. I was a dick. Okay? I'm sorry."

"No. It's not that. I'm pregnant."

"What?" He raised his eyebrows. "You're kidding, right?"

She didn't respond and lowered her head.

He shook his head as his face turned red. "What the hell? How? You told me you are on the pill! You know we can't keep it."

"Relax, it's not yours, and please don't tell me whether I should keep the baby or not. It's not your decision," she said in an icy tone.

He clenched his fist and got off the bed. "You're right. I'm sorry. How long have you known?" He started pacing the room

"For a while."

He stopped pacing, and he turned to face her. "What the fuck? Why did you still sleep with me when you knew you were pregnant?"

She got silent for a bit and looked around the room. Tears rolled down her cheeks. "I know it was a shitty thing to do. I couldn't control myself. Can we go home now? I don't want to talk about this further."

Karma suddenly couldn't stand looking at him anymore. A sudden sense of doom descended on her like a heavy black cloud that signaled a strong storm. She felt disgusted by him, by herself, by the whole situation. She felt guilty for everything she had done. For cheating on her husband, for the constant lies, and for endangering her baby by having unprotected sex with a random dude who happened to live in her neighborhood.

She felt nauseous.

"Hey. Wait. Please wait. I still want to see you. I don't care that you're pregnant. I really enjoy our time together." His voice was earnest.

She clenched her jaw tightly. "I want to leave now. If you don't drive me now, I'll get an Uber instead."

"Okay. Okay." He got off the bed.

On the way back home, they were mostly silent. She couldn't look him in the eyes. *How did I even find him attractive?* She hated how he always smelled of cigarettes, that his teeth were yellow, and that the front one was chipped. She hated that he hardly shaved. That his clothes were always wrinkled. She hated his uncircumcised penis. She mostly loathed the fact that he didn't even offer to split the cost of the cabin with her. *What kind of man is he?*

As the woods gave way to urban landscapes, she contemplated confessing everything to Jamal and asking for his forgiveness. They could start over, open a new chapter. He'd need to stop seeing Gina, and they could raise their child happily and forget about what they both had done.

There was still a chance to save her marriage, to save her family, to give her son a happy start.

Vadim dropped her off at the church parking lot, and then she walked back home, replaying the scenes of her time in the cabin with her lover: the horrible hike, the time in the bathtub, and his whining.

What have I done?

She felt bile rise to her throat and had to stop herself from throwing up.

When she got home, Jamal was eating a turkey sandwich by the kitchen counter. Baladi got off the sofa and jumped to greet her, licking her face.

"Looks like you had fun," said Jamal after giving her a quick kiss on the cheek

"Yeah," she said, happy to be home, mad at herself for being so mean to Jamal the last few months.

"The place looked amazing," he said. "Do you feel refreshed?"

"I do," she lied. "I missed you a lot." She gave him a long hug. "It was our first night not being in bed together," she said. "I don't want it to happen again. Sleeping without you is not fun."

She meant it, but guilt started creeping in. *What the hell have I done? Who was this person she was becoming?*

That night, they both sat in bed, reading. Karma pretended to read a romance novel while Jamal read a magazine. She had to approach the topic, but she didn't know how; instead, she decided to smooth things over by sleeping with him. She put her book on the nightstand and kissed him.

He stopped her. "First things first, can we talk about Vadim?"

Chapter 13

IT WAS THE longest night of Karma's life, one that she would never forget, one that would leave many permanent scars.

"Vadim, who?" she said, her beating heart threatening to jump from her chest. Jamal rolled his eyes. "Okay. Let me try again. Vadim, the neighbor you meet for coffee," he said, making air quotes with his fingers. "Does that ring a bell?"

Karma couldn't breathe. She felt dizzy.

"Vadim, the one that you walk with to the woods to do God knows what. What a romantic stop you both chose! Didn't know you had it in you," he snickered.

Karma opened her mouth and tried to speak, but couldn't. She felt paralyzed. She closed her mouth and suddenly felt her throat was dry. She needed water. She swallowed.

"Did I jog your memory, my love?" he asked, shaking his head. A faint smile crossed his face, one of triumph. She stayed silent.

They were both sitting up in bed, illuminated by the light from their bedside tables.

"No?" He tilted his head. "You still don't know who I'm talking about? You still have no clue?" asked Jamal. "What's wrong? Your face turned pale suddenly. Are my questions bothering you, my dear?"

The tone of his voice took Karma aback. The sarcasm, the hidden rage, the snide words. Who was that man sitting beside her? That was not the man she married, the man she lost her virginity to, the man she'd slept next to for almost two years. He'd never spoken to her like that before.

He leaned back, arms crossed, a cold smirk twisting his lips. "Let me see. Ah. The guy you spent the weekend with in a cabin by the fireplace in the mountains?"

Karma exploded in tears. "I'm sorry. I'm so sorry. I'm terrible, terrible. Please forgive me. I was not myself. I was tricked. El Sheitan got in my head! The devil! He made me do all these vile things!"

"The devil?" he chuckled. "I see. Ah! How convenient. Let's blame it on the devil. Who convinced you to say that? Your mom? Did she write your talking points?"

"You gotta believe me. It's complicated..." she pleaded. "I already recognized my mistake, and I ended things with him. I'll never see him again. Please forgive me. I love you. I love our baby. Let's put this behind us."

"Really? How stupid you are, Karma." His chuckle was hollow. "You think I can just forgive and forget and move on? I knew you were stupid when I first met you, but I married you anyway." He shook his head slowly.

She struggled to breathe as she felt a knife being jammed into her heart.

"I'm really sorry. I'll do anything you want. I'll be the best wife and the best mom."

He let out a dry laugh. "Seriously? What kind of a man do you think I am, ha? Do you think I can just forgive you for screwing a man while you're pregnant with my son? Sucking his dick in the woods! You're a slut. That's what you are. You're nothing more than a slut that I bought from Bilaq. I could have picked any slut I wanted, but for some reason, I picked the worst of them all."

Her life was falling apart before her eyes. "Stop it, please, Jamal. Stop saying these horrible things to me."

He scoffed. "Really? Horrible things? Let me ask you something. Did he go down on you?"

"Please stop," she pleaded in between her sobs.

"Answer me!" he shouted. "Did he go down on you?"

She covered her face with her hands. "Stop!"

He grabbed her wrist so hard she felt her bones breaking.

"You're hurting me. Stop!"

"I'm hurting you? Good. I want to keep hurting you. I want you to scream in pain. I want the whole neighborhood to hear your shouts. They have already heard your moans of pleasure, ya sharmouta. They might as well hear your screams! Answer me now! Answer me!"

"Yes," she whispered.

He shook his head. "As I expected. You're nothing but a slut, a whore, a cunt!"

"Enough!" she snapped. "Stop it, Jamal. Stop saying these words. What difference does it make? Sex is sex. Whether he fucks me or goes down on me!"

That's when she felt his slap on her cheek and screamed in pain. A sharp cramp in her stomach followed, and she shrieked. "You monster! You hit me!" She felt her cheek numb from the pain and couldn't open her jaw.

Jamal's face didn't change; there was no remorse, just rage.

"It's not like you never screwed around, you liar," she said, surprised by the vulgar words coming out of her mouth in front of her husband—that enraged enigma, who could easily break her bones and crush her skull.

He let go of her wrist. "What the fuck are you talking about? You'll never find a better husband than me —a better provider, a better partner. I gave you everything you wanted. Everything! Look around you. Look at the house. Look at your house. Everything you have is because of me!"

"You're cheating on me!" she yelled.

He scoffed. "Seriously? Are you accusing me of cheating? What a cheap shot. And who told you that? Was it also the devil? Did your mom tell you to say that, too?"

Her lips trembled. "Please don't ask me how I know. It's hard to explain."

"You're a bitch. Just a pathetic excuse for a human being. I can't believe you would accuse me of that when you are the one who is whoring around the neighborhood."

Jamal got out of bed, quickly picked a pair of pants and a shirt from the closet, put them on, and left the room.

"Jamal, wait, please wait," she said, shooting out of bed and running down the stairs after him.

Baladi got off the sofa in the living room and trotted after Jamal, who left the house, slamming the front door behind him. Karma felt a sharp pain in her stomach as she heard him drive his car away from their house, away from her.

Karma went back to her bedroom and wailed, hugging the pillow. She couldn't believe the awful things he had said, how he'd hurt her, slapped her, and grabbed her wrist as if he intentionally wanted to squeeze her until she bled. She was married to a wife-beater. How could this be? How did I allow this to happen?

She cried and thought about her life, about what had transpired the past few years—meeting Jamal, getting engaged, getting married, moving to the US, getting Baladi, getting pregnant, Vadim, Danielle. Her visions. Oh, her visions. They caused her so much pain, so much heartache, so much anguish. Suddenly, she was gasping for air.

She grabbed her phone from the bedside table and called her mom. It was just after 5:00 a.m. in Bilaq, but she didn't care.

After two rings, her mom picked up. "Why are you calling at this hour?" her mom asked by way of greeting. "Are you okay? Is Jamal okay?"

As soon as she heard her mom's voice, Karma started wailing.

Karma's mom gasped. "What is it? Who died?"

"No one died, Mama," she said between her sobs.

"What's the matter then? Tell me, ya binit?" Her mother raised her voice.

"It's Jamal. I know now for sure that he's cheating." Karma couldn't bring herself to tell her mom the whole story—her affair, the sins she had already committed—so she just focused on Jamal's transgression.

Her mom remained silent.

"Hello, Mama! Did you hear me? Jamal is cheating," said Karma, raising her voice.

Her mom sighed over the phone. "Is that it?" her mom asked.

"Yes, that's it," Karma said in a sharp tone.

Karma's mom let out a long sigh.

"Mom, are you there?" Karma could hear her mom's heavy breathing.

"I'm here. Listen, habeebti, all men cheat. We already talked about it. Not a huge deal. And how do you know he's cheating?"

"Mama. It is a huge deal," Karma said, raising her voice. "And I know he's cheating."

"How do you know? Did you see him in bed with her?" she said in a skeptical tone.

"No!"

"Do you have evidence? Emails, letters, texts?"

"No."

"Did he come home smelling of another woman's perfume? Perhaps a lipstick smudge on his shirt collar?"

"No."

She rolled her eyes. "Seriously, Karma. Then how do you know?"

Karma hesitated for a moment, then said, "I had a vision."

"Really, Karma? Again? How many times?" Karma's mom shouted into the phone. "How many times did I tell you to stop that nonsense? You're going to ruin your life with those stupid visions! They don't mean anything. Focus on your husband, your baby, and stop with these silly thoughts. Stop it, now, Karma, or I will jump on the nearest flight and deal with you myself. You're going to ruin everything. Your husband will divorce you. Stop this now!"

Karma pressed on her teeth. "Mama, I have to go." Karma hung up the phone.

What would her mom say if she found out that Karma was also cheating? Would she be that dismissive of her cheating? Would she reciprocate the sentiment, accept it the way she wanted Karma to accept Jamal's transgressions? Would she say women also need to distribute their eggs the same way men have the urge to spread their seed? Bullshit! She would immediately disown Karma if she found out. She would call her a sharmouta, a whore. Gahbeh, a bigger whore.

She slipped under the down comforter, wanting to disappear forever.

Why did she even listen to her visions? Why did she let them guide her life? All her efforts to suppress them had failed; they always managed to find a way to appear, to emerge uninvited.

Her visions had never disappointed her before, always coming true. Her vision in which Jamal was screwing Gina was bound to be accurate. Why wouldn't it be? Why did Jamal deny it? To make her feel guilty about what she had done? Even Danielle had confirmed it.

Suddenly, something clicked in Karma's mind. She felt as if a bolt of lightning had just hit her. Instantly, everything fell into place. She sat up in bed and gasped. Danielle confirmed the vision, but she didn't confirm the time! The vision was for the future. The vision is yet to happen, but Danielle has made me believe it has already happened.

That bitch!

She messed up my head. She made me lose my bearings. My visions always show the future, not the present. That demon made me think his cheating was already happening. She messed up my visions, the only thing that was functioning in my life the way it should be.

KARMA DIDN'T SLEEP a single minute. She stayed up all night fuming, an entangled mess of guilt, of shame, of sadness, of rage. She wanted to smash walls and throw furniture. She worried about how all this stress would affect the baby. She had read many internet articles about the effect a mother's stress could have, forcing the child into earlier delivery or having a low birth weight. Her poor baby. What kind of life awaited him now that his mom had messed up their family?

It was all her fault. She was selfish and vile. She was a whore. A sharmouta. Would Jamal ever forgive her? Would he even come back? Did she even want him back now that she had seen a different side of him, a monstrous side? She didn't know what to think anymore. She felt untethered from her values. Ungrounded and afraid.

As soon as the sun came out, she washed her face, dressed, grabbed Baladi, and walked to Danielle's house. She wanted to catch her before she headed to school—that's if the witch ever went to school. She wanted to grab Danielle and tear out all her hair. She wanted to scratch her face until she screamed. She wanted to break all her bones and hear her shriek in excruciating pain.

She ran out of the house so quickly that she forgot to get her hat and gloves. It was a frigid, dry, late winter day. As she walked, snowflakes fell on her head. She put her hands in her parka pocket while holding Baladi's leash and kept walking.

When Danielle emerged from the house, looking sleepy and annoyed with a backpack strapped to one shoulder, Karma was waiting for her on the sidewalk across from her house.

Baladi barked at the sight of her.

Danielle walked to the dog and put her hand on his head. Baladi stopped barking.

"What's the matter?" asked Danielle, looking at Karma. "Love troubles? You look like shit!"

Karma had to stop herself from lunging at her. "You're a liar. You deceived me and ruined my marriage. You planted a thought in my head that he was cheating." Karma was hyperventilating.

Danielle smiled. "Oh, did I? Weren't you the one who had the vision?" She pulled a vape from the pocket of her black jeans and took a puff.

"The vision has not happened yet. You convinced me to cheat on Jamal as revenge. He has been loyal all this time," Karma said, pointing a finger at her.

Danielle exhaled vapor and then made a tsk sound. "Oh, please. Didn't I tell you to stop being I, especially about men? What difference does it make, ha?! He's a cheater. He'll always be. Cheating now or cheating later is the same."

"No. It's not!" Karma said, dizzied by the smell of rosewater emanating from Danielle.

Danielle leaned in closer. "Really? Where do you think he is now? He spent the night with Gina, you fool!"

"Come on! No, he didn't," Karma said, trying to maintain her balance. She focused her attention on Danielle's red Converse shoes, unable to look her in the eyes. The girl, the witch, had an uncontrollable power over her.

"Fine. Stay in denial," Danielle said slowly as if making a point.

Baladi stood up and barked at a passing wild rabbit. Karma pointed her finger at him, and he immediately stopped barking. "If he did," she said to Danielle, "then I pushed him to do that. I drove him to it. I listened to your bullshit."

"Here we go with the victim-blaming. And, honey, what's that red spot on your cheek? Looks like he roughed you up." Danielle took a step closer and ran her fingers on Karma's cheek. Karma felt goosebumps on her arms. "I hope you fought back," she said, stroking her cheek.

"Stay the fuck away from me. Don't you ever touch me!" shouted Karma as she jumped back. "You ruined my family."

Danielle shook her head. "Oh, please. Do you even know anything about your husband? Do you really know him at all?"

Karma closed her eyes, and when she opened them, her vision was blurry. She couldn't see Danielle's face anymore. The world before her seemed to dissolve into a mist, thick and swirling with shades of silver and gray. She closed her eyes again, and when she opened them this time, Danielle was not there; instead, a voluptuous woman with big brown eyes and curly red hair stood before her. She was wearing a long, flowy dress that showed her cleavage. Warped around her arm was a black snake, and she held a yellow flower in her hand. Karma shrieked. The red-headed woman disappeared, and instead, Karma was faced again with Danielle.

Who was that? Lilith? Did she summon her?

"Hey, hey," said Danielle. "No need for all that shouting. You don't want the neighbors to notice, do you?" she said as a couple with a toddler passed by them.

"What are you saying, you crazy witch? What are you saying about my husband?" Karma asked, shaking her head.

"Do you really think he's a surgeon?"

Karma let out a quick bark of laughter. "Of course, he's a surgeon! What do you think he does for a living, drive an Uber?"

Danielle raised her eyebrows. "You're so naïve and a classist, too. How many times did you go with him to work?"

Karma, momentarily taken aback, quickly recovered. "He works at Saint Jude Hospital. We passed by it many times. He even showed me where his office is located!"

Danielle sighed. "You stupid woman! Have you been inside his office?"

Karma bit back her words. She hadn't.

"My dear, I hate to break it to you, but being a surgeon is his cover," said Danielle with a smirk.

"His cover?" asked Karma, tilting her head.

"Yes, honey," said Danielle as she inhaled from her vape. "He's a CIA agent. He's a fucking spy."

Karma gasped. "What? What are you saying? You're lying. You lie all the time!"

"The CIA has hired him to spy on you. All of it—the marriage, the house, the baby—all of it is a cover. Your marriage is a fucking sham," she said calmly as if discussing the weather.

"Stop it. Please stop it. You're lying." Her voice trembled. "Why would he spy on me? What do I have to offer? I'm just a woman from a middle-class family in Bilaq."

"Okay, I have some homework for you. When you get home, please Google "Project Stargate.""

"I'm not Googling shit. You're crazy!" Karma heard herself shouting and worried she was making a scene in the neighborhood.

"Listen, honey, you have psychic ability and speak Arabic. You're the perfect recruit for the US government."

"Seriously? You're a CIA expert now?" she said, then felt a cramp. She kept the grimace off her face, not wanting Danielle to detect her agony.

Danielle ignored her comment and kept talking. "Project Stargate was a bust, and the government had to shut it down. But now they're recreating it." She adjusted her backpack on her shoulder. "They want it better and bigger, and you fit all the criteria. They want to test your ability to predict the enemy's moves remotely before they happen."

Karma's skin tingled. "What enemy?"

"Extremists, especially those who speak Arabic. ISIS, Al Qaeda, Hamas, whatever. Not only can you see and predict their moves, but you can also speak their language and understand their culture. Jamal marrying you is the perfect plan. He can monitor you, keep tabs on you, groom you, and report back to his supervisor. He's a brilliant spy. Not even his mom knows what he does for a living." Dan'elle's tone was matter-of-fact, almost clinical, as she unloaded this barrage of information.

Karma couldn't breathe and felt her hands trembling. She remembered her conversation with Jamal's mom when they first visited and how she told her that Jamal was one of the best surgeons in the U.S.

Did he lie to his mom, too?

"Do you think he picked this neighborhood randomly? Or the street you live on. Jasmine Drive? Really? Of all the names of the streets in suburbia, he picked Jasmine Drive, the flower symbol of your country. Why? Just to make you happy? For its nice curbside appeal? Everything he does is meticulously planned. Open your fucking eyes. A lot is happening in this neighborhood that you know nothing about." She looked around the street. "You're just a work assignment to him. Nothing but a guinea pig in an interesting experiment that might get him a promotion."

"Shut up!" she blurted, fists clenched at her sides, fighting back tears.

"And that annoying dog of yours," Danielle said, pointing at Baladi. "Do you think he got him because you were lonely? Honey, this dog has a GPS chip embedded in him. Jamal monitors all your moves."

Karma couldn't take it anymore; she could hardly breathe. She grabbed Baladi and turned to head home.

"Just Google Project Stargate," Danielle yelled as Karma walked away, tears streaming down her face.

It couldn't be true. Jamal, her Jamal, a spy? The CIA knew about her visions. And where was Jamal now? Was he even upset about the cheating, or was that all an act?

"You're nothing but a guinea pig," she heard Danielle say in her head.

A sharp cramp doubled her over in pain; she let out a shrill cry. She stopped for a moment and took a deep breath as she waited for the pain to go away.

As she resumed walking home, she remembered the first time she had asked Jamal about Jasmine Drive.

"Wow, Jasmine Drive. What a nice name!" she'd said when he took her to see their house for the first time. It was the same day he picked her up from the airport after she left Bilaq and headed to the US for the first time, having finalized her immigration papers. "Did you pick that street just for me?" she'd asked, looking around at all the other single-family homes in her new neighborhood.

"It just worked out this way," he'd said. "I'm glad it made you happy." He kissed her forehead. "Now let me show you inside the house. You'll love it."

WHEN KARMA GOT home after her encounter with Danielle, she went upstairs to the bedroom, got under the covers, and cried herself to sleep. She wanted to call her mom and confess everything about Vadim, Danielle, and her husband, the spy.

Then, she would beg her forgiveness and ask her to take her back to her home in Bilaq, where she would savor the taste of Turkish coffee in the morning and the soothing scent of sage tea in the afternoon, accompanied by the sound of the Azan announcing the evening prayers and the fragrance of Jasmine flowers in the neighborhood's streets.

To the people smoking argeeleh in the evening and kids staying up past midnight. To drink hot tea for breakfast and snack on raw cucumbers in the afternoon. To the morning sounds of pigeons taking shelter on the roof of her building, to having knaffeh and fresh fruit for dessert. To the sight of stray cats wandering the street with no aim in the world. To people smoking right under the no-smoking signs.

Driving to the red desert in the winter while dodging camels as they cross the street. To the sight of the coffee boy selling Arabic coffee by the side of the highway. To use the metric system. Saying football, not soccer. Watching Egyptian movies with her mom. Dealing with traffic jams and people not stopping at stop signs. To people showing up uninvited at your house at any time of the day. Having dinner after 10:00 PM. Touching people and getting close to them without worrying about their personal space. To the dread of regional conflict looming in the air. Observing people roaming around the streets with nothing to do. Experiencing catcallers admiring her body. She ached to be home with its good and bad, away from that foreign land and its indecipherable creatures.

When she woke up, she checked her phone. Nothing from Jamal. Instead, there was a text from Vadim:

Vadim: Can we talk?

She deleted it. She didn't have time for him now.

She opened her phone browser and typed "Project Stargate." The first result was from Wikipedia. Stargate Project was the 1991 code name for a secret U.S. Army unit established in 1978 at Fort Meade, Maryland, by the Defense Intelligence Agency and SRI International to investigate the potential for psychic phenomena in military and domestic intelligence applications.

Her heart dropped. Could Danielle be right?

She kept on reading. She found an article titled "The CIA Recruited' Mind Readers' to Spy on the Soviets in the 1970s."

Psychics helped with top-secret programs.

Army veteran Joseph McMoneagle stood out among the remote viewers who worked with the government's top-secret program. As he later told The Washington Post, McMoneagle was involved in approximately 450 missions between 1978 and 1984, including helping the Army locate hostages in Iran and guiding CIA agents to a shortwave radio concealed in the pocket calculator of a suspected KGB agent captured in South Africa.

Karma's head was spinning. Remote viewing? Wasn't that what Danielle had mentioned? Was that what they called visions in the CIA language?

And people like me are called remote viewers? Was I a remote viewer?

She looked at Baladi, sleeping on the floor beside her. She ran her hand over his back, trying to feel the GPS chip Danielle had mentioned. I' can't be true. Baladi, her Baladi is part of a bigger scheme against her?

She paced around the room. She was losing every single cell left in her brain.

She headed to the bed and, with her shaking hands, pulled one of the journals from underneath the mattress. Maybe she would find answers.

Sometimes, I dream about leaving Bilaq. I dream of going far, far away, to a place where no one knows my name, where no one knows my language, where no one cares about my culture, my traditions, my social boundaries, or my taboos —a place like America, the land of the free. Would I be accepted there? Would they have doctors there who specialized in my case? They must. After all, they managed to put a man on the moon. They can do anything. They should be able to fix me. Would they put me in a lab and analyze me? Or would they just let me go? Would they let me live freely, just the way I am? Would I be happier there, in a land that is not my own? Would I be satisfied if I, the Misfit, tried to fit in the land where everything goes?

Karma closed the journal with her trembling hand.

How naive this woman is. No one can cure people like us. Not even in the land of the free.

Chapter 14

A GUINEA PIG, KARMA thought. I'm nothing but a guinea pig. Tears fell down her cheeks. She put the journal away and started rocking back and forth like a dervish dancer.

She was losing her mind. She had to find out if what Danielle had told her was true.

Was her husband a spy?

Karma manically rummaged through Jamal's drawers in their bedroom, looking for hidden clues and proof of his clandestine activities. Nothing. All she found were his Calvin Klein boxers, socks, ties, and undershirts.

She went downstairs to his basement office, feeling shortness of breath followed by a mild cramp, but she ignored her physical symptoms and focused on the task ahead.

She opened his laptop and tried to log in, but couldn't figure out the password. Of course, he would have a complicated password like a good spy!

On the desk were a few bills. Electricity, water, and gas. A cup of pens and a stapler were also present. She opened the drawers, finding more bills and receipts, as well as a couple of stamp albums. She'd had no idea he collected stamps. What else didn't she know about him?

Everything was organized, and the rest of the drawers were mostly empty.

She took the drawers out, flipped them over, and looked underneath, hoping to find something taped there—a key to a deposit box, just like in the movies.

Nothing.

Everything was just too neat.

She went upstairs to the living room and removed some of the framed photos from the walls, searching for a hidden case, just like she had read in mystery books.

Nothing!

She closed her eyes, cleared her mind, and recalled all the James Bond movies she had watched through the years. Didn't 007 have an escape bag stashed with cash and multiple passports? Where did he hide it? Would it be in an air vent?

She opened the back porch and walked to the end of the backyard toward the wooden shed. The door was already unlocked.

Once inside, she found Jamal's toolbox on top of his wooden workbench.

She rummaged through his toolbox and grabbed every screwdriver she could find, then headed back to the house. The first air duct was located in the kitchen, so she tried several screwdrivers before one finally worked.

She stuck her hand inside the vent.

Nothing but dust.

She searched the entire house, locating and unscrewing every air duct she could find.

She was losing her fucking mind.

Her back hurt, and she was having minor cramps—Braxton hicks, or whatever the hell they called them. Or was she losing the baby?

God was punishing her. He was going to take her baby away.

She started to feel shortness of breath again and began to shake.

Right. When was the last time she'd eaten?

She went to the kitchen and ate Labneh on pita bread as she thought of her parents and how much she missed them. Tears streamed down her face as she ached to be with them at this moment, to be on the living room sofa, drinking mint tea with her dad as they watched the news on Al Jazeera and chatted about the region's affairs. Why did she even agree to get married in the first place? She was miserable. She'd rather be a spinster, a pariah, than remain stuck in her current status—married to a man she didn't know, who was a cheater and a liar living a double life. She didn't deserve to bring children into this world. God was right to punish me, she thought as her heart started to palpitate, and her chest felt tight.

She went upstairs and sighed, needing to find an answer.

She lifted the mattress, picked one of the journals, and flipped through the pages. She then skipped to the last page, hoping that the previous one might contain what she was looking for.

Today is my wedding day. I'm so terrified. Not about losing my virginity, not at all. I know the process will hurt, but women tolerate that all the time. Yeah, yeah, some end up hospitalized, but eventually, they survive their wedding night and end up bearing many children. I'll be okay. I know I won't orgasm on my wedding night. No woman does, from my understanding. I'm not worried about that. After all, I know how to pleasure myself. I have been doing it for years.

I'm just so scared that he will find out about my true evil nature. Of all the people who came to ask for my hand in marriage, he was the only one who didn't cause me to have visions. I liked that. He was an enigma. I wanted the excitement. I wanted to look forward to our lives together, to anticipate the future instead of dreading it. He is a kind, loving, good provider, and even funny. He always makes me laugh. I know he would make me happy and would give me good children, but what if he found out about my secret? What if I see a vision while he makes me a woman on our wedding night, and I freak out and confess? Would he be scared of me? Would he think I'm deformed? Would he call me el Jenyeeh and send me back to my parents' house? Would I become returned goods, already open and already used, unwanted forever?

I can't afford to lose him. Oh, God, oh, dear God, please have mercy on me. Let me have this one thing in my life. You made me this way, please, oh God, oh merciful. Let me have a happy marriage. I promise I will be better. I promise. I will control my evil thoughts. I will control my visions. I will do my best to stop them when they come. I will squeeze my brain so hard to make them go away. I will work so hard not to enjoy seeing evil or death. I will be good. I promise—no more visions for me. I will do my best. Just let me keep him. Let me keep my man.

Karma felt a knot in her stomach. The woman's plea was so similar to hers; her desperation was the same.

How many of us are out there?

Karma tucked the journal underneath the bed and pulled out her phone. She was finally going to do it: search the Internet to find out how many there were.

Her mom had already warned her about leaving breadcrumbs about her condition. "Don't you go searching on the computer and use that Google thing," her mom told her when she got married. "Jamal would find out," she told her. "Keep your secret hidden. I have no idea how I bore a child with your condition, but what can we do? This is what God gave me!"

Even before she got married, Karma had attempted to research her condition to unravel its mystery, but she got scared at the last minute and closed her computer right after she opened the search engine. Her mom warned her that the Mukhabarat, the intelligence police, monitored the internet, and if they found out about her condition, she might be questioned and even imprisoned.

"Don't leave breadcrumbs," her mom's words always resonated in her ears.

Karma didn't care anymore. Everything was fucked. Everything. Breadcrumbs or not. She no longer cared. He could find out about her secret. The police could grab her. She tapped on her phone with her thumb and finally googled: People who see future visions.

Her jaw dropped as she marveled at the number of hits.

There were documented cases. Everywhere. She was not crazy.

She found an article in the New Yorker magazine, a publication she had never heard of before, about a British doctor who collected stories of visions in the Welsh village of Aberfan, which was the site of the collapse of a colliery spoil tip, whatever the hell that means, in 1966 that killed 116 children and 28 adults after it engulfed a school and several houses.

According to the article she read, the British psychiatrist John Barker noticed "several strange and pathetic incidents" connected with the coal slip. "Bereaved families spoke of dreams and prophecies. On the eve of the disaster, an eight-year-old boy named Paul Davies had drawn massed figures digging in the hillside under the words 'the end.'"

Another story Baker collected was about a ten-year-old girl. The day before the disaster, she said to her mother, "Mummy, let me tell you about my dream last night." Her mother answered gently, "Darling, I've no time. Tell me again later." The child replied, "No, Mummy, you must listen. I dreamt I went to school, and there was no school there. Something black had come down all over it!"

Karma suddenly felt a splitting headache; all her life, she'd thought she was crazy, deformed, and born with an incurable mental illness.

She was not insane or damaged; she had a superpower.

Her headache got stronger. She closed her eyes, trying to numb the throbbing pain, and thought about what she had read. She slowly drifted to sleep, dreaming of meeting those other people scattered all over the globe—those who had visions, those who wrote journals about their unique experiences, and those who were not crazy—those who were exceptional, super special.

WHEN SHE OPENED her eyes, Jamal was sitting up in bed beside her, looking at his phone. Her heart dropped. She tried to say something, but she couldn't find any words. She was not sure what to feel. Guilt, shame, or anger. Should she trust him? Did he spend the night at Gina's, like what Danielle told her? She didn't know what to believe anymore.

"Hey," he said, stroking her forehead. "You feel rested?"

She was stunned by the display of affection. "Yeah. A bit."

"We need to talk," he said. He was very calm, a totally different person from the night before, as if he had just taken a tranquilizer. "I'm sorry about what I said last night." He looked tired, and his eyes were teary.

Should I believe him?

His voice wavered slightly. "You know I didn't mean what I said. I was just upset. You know, I love you very much."

Karma kept quiet.

"I just couldn't believe you would do this to me. I never expected it from you." He let out a long sigh. "I thought we had a great marriage, and I did my best to be a good husband, but I think I have been very neglectful. I spent most of my time working and didn't pay you any attention. Women have needs, too, you know, and I totally ignored that. I can take responsibility for that."

He looked at her intently, then held her hand. "I want to forgive you, and I want us to start fresh for the sake of our baby. I'm not sure things will be the same as they were before because I have a lot of anger inside me, but I'll try to put it behind me and move on for the sake of our son, for the sake of our marriage, and for the sake of our family."

Karma opened her mouth and then closed it again.

His voice broke slightly. "I'm so sorry I hit you. I just couldn't control my anger. I snapped. That was not me. I'll never lay a finger on you ever again."

Was that part of his spy training?

He looked at her intently. "You know, we had a good marriage. A perfect marriage. I don't want to flush what we had down the toilet. I want to give it one more try before I end us. I love us."

The CIA wrote this script for him. It's just too good.

"I'm sorry," she finally said. "I really am."

He kissed her hand, but she felt nothing. He smelled of sweat, and she suddenly felt nauseous.

"Let's start fresh, and to prove it, I just asked my boss for a sabbatical." He gave her hand another kiss.

"What does that mean?" she asked, pulling her hand back.

"It means I'll be staying home. I'm no longer going to the hospital. I'll be around all the time to help out with the baby and keep you company." His eyes were earnest.

She swallowed. "What about all your patients?" At that fake hospital and the fake job of yours, you asshole!

"You and the baby are more important." He took a strand of her hair between his fingers and sniffed it. "You smell nice as always!"

Oh god, he wants to be around to watch me. To record my every move and send his reports. "What about the money?" she said, almost whispering. She was scared of unleashing his anger. She was worried he would hit her again. He might hit her and the baby.

He might kill them both.

He gave her a half smile. "Ah, baby. Don't worry about that. I always provide. You know that."

He really is a spy. Danielle was right. Danielle was always right.

Karma felt a cramp followed by a sharp pain in her back. She moaned.

His face softened. "Baby. Are you okay?"

"Just a cramp. It's normal in the third trimester," she said, squinting, placing a hand on her belly.

BUT OVER THE next few hours, her cramps started getting closer to each other, and Jamal suggested calling Dr. Grahm.

"Dr. Grahm said we should take you to the ER," Jamal said after getting off the phone.

"What? I still have months left," she said, "Maybe four." Then she felt a sharp pain.

"You might be in labor," he said, pacing back and forth around the room.

"No, it's early. It can't be," she started sobbing. "Please stop pacing. You're making it hard for me to relax."

She let out a wail.

"We have to leave now. We can't have the baby in this house." He reached her side of the bed, grabbed her hand, and started helping her get up.

Tears streamed down her face. "I'm not leaving. We're not having the baby now! I don't even have a bag ready."

"Baby, don't worry about it. I'll take care of that later. Now we need to get you to the ER."

"Please call my mom," begged Karma. "Call her now. Tell her to come here. To take the first flight. I need her now." Karma wailed nonstop.

"I will, baby, I will."

On the way to the hospital, Karma shrieked from pain and cried from fear. In between her shouts, she noticed that Jamal was taking a different and longer route to the hospital.

"Where are we going?" she asked, then let out a moan.

"To the hospital," he said. "Where do you think we are going?" He clutched the steering wheel with both hands.

"Which hospital?"

"Suburban," he said quietly, almost whispering.

Her chest tightened. "Suburban hospital? Why? Why not St. Jude?"

"Suburban is better, trust me."

She could see beads of sweat forming on his forehead. "What? But that's not where you work. That's not where Dr. Grahm works!"

"Please stop talking. I need to focus on driving us safely there."

She felt her body shaking. "You told me it's better if we go to St. Jude, that everyone knows you there, and they'll give me special treatment."

"Trust me, okay?" he said, his eyes fixed on the road.

"Trust you?" she shouted. "I don't even know you! What are you hiding from me? Do you even work at St. Jude?"

He sighed. "Karma. You're hysterical and in a lot of pain. Please take a deep breath."

"Get me out of the car!" she shrieked. "I don't want to be with you now! Where are you taking me? Get me out. Get me the fuck out!" She started banging on the window. "Help! Get me out of here. Help me! Someone help me!"

"Karma, shut the fuck up, okay?" he raised his voice. "We're almost there."

When she arrived at the hospital, she was depleted, like she would die any moment. She couldn't take the pain and was paralyzed in fear. Two nurses at the emergency entrance greeted her before rolling her into triage—a large, brightly lit room with multiple beds separated by thin, green curtains.

The nurse who examined her was young and blonde. She had a long medieval sword tattoo on her arm and multiple ear piercings.

"I don't want to be here," shouted Karma. "What's this place? I should be at St. Jude, where my doctor works. Not here. My husband dragged me here."

The nurse ignored her and kept examining her.

"You're 10 centimeters dilated," said the nurse calmly, her voice hoarse. "Buckle up! The baby is coming soon."

Jamal squeezed her hand, but she pulled it back.

The next few hours were all a daze. Nurses coming in and out, needles in and out. They hooked her up to several machines and spread her legs apart. Many people appeared, poking at her insides, hands inside her vagina. Blood and cramps and pain—excruciating pain.

Some nurses' touches triggered visions, others didn't. Her brain was a mosaic of visions, coming in and out, each one overlapping. She was unsure if she was hallucinating from pain or if the visions were real. They just kept on coming.

She saw one nurse on a beach on a tropical island sipping a cocktail; she saw another nurse snorting cocaine in a public bathroom. One nurse was slitting her wrists, while another walked down the aisle of a church dressed in white, her father by her side. She saw a male doctor making love to another man. She saw a female doctor dead from a gunshot wound to the head.

Pain, contractions, blood, lots of blood. One vision after another. She closed her eyes and wanted it all to end. She rubbed her forehead and continued to rub it until she shrieked. Please, stop! she commanded her visions. I want out of this nightmare.

"Is she okay?" she heard Jamal ask the nurse.

"Yes. She is just in pain. Totally normal."

"I don't want that baby anymore. I don't want him. Take him away," she kept shouting.

"They all say that," said the nurse, smiling and looking at Jamal. "Just wait, and she will start calling you names soon."

Karma could hear the nurse laugh. Fuck her.

Jamal placed his hand on Karma's. "Shhhh," he said in a calming voice.

She closed her eyes and began to daydream of happier times, walking with her dad on a Friday morning to grab hummus and falafel from the neighborhood shop down the street, or sitting on the veranda with her friend Najah as they watched neighbors pass by, cracking open watermelon seeds with their teeth and listening to Amr Diab blast from a small, Chinese-made boombox.

When she finally reopened her eyes, one of the doctors was looking at her intensely. She heard a deep, manly voice. "Can you hear me, Mrs. Ibrahim? Can you hear me?"

Karma's life suddenly flashed in front of her. Her mom, her dad. Running in the streets of Bilaq. Drinking juice with the neighbor as they watched the boys across the street, play soccer, and lamenting the fact that girls like them were not allowed to play soccer. Finding out her cousin Khaled was gay after seeing a vision of him kissing the son of the grocer. Her university days. The creepy professor who grabbed her boobs when she stopped by his office. The first political rally she had ever taken part in. The first man who held her hand and caused her to see unflattering images of him. Going to her friend's wedding and wondering if she would ever get married.

Jamal is visiting her house for the first time. On her wedding day, seeing a penis for the first time. Losing her virginity. The pain. The blood on the sheets. Her first orgasm. The waves of pleasure. Moving to her new house. Jasmine Drive. Hating the furniture Jamal picked for her. Walking Baladi. Her plants. The black-eyed Susan. Veronica. Dom. Dom is hanging from a rope.

Jill, her three-legged dog Mia. Hunting for furniture with her. The fight in the woods. Her broken arm.

Brent, the hot windows salesman. The journals. That woman in the journal. Vadim. The woods. The Red Converse shoes. Rosewater.

Danielle. Danielle. Danielle.

She needed Danielle, the only one who could help her. She and Danielle were made from the same material. They were not mere flesh and blood; they were much, much more than that. They were creatures from another dimension.

Where is Danielle?

"We need to intervene now," the doctor said. "We might lose both of them."

A MIDDLE-AGED NURSE named Carla solemnly wheeled Karma to the NICU to see the baby.

"Is the baby okay?" asked Karma.

After three hours of pushing, the baby's heartbeat had dropped to a dangerous level, and she was rushed to the operating room for a C-section. Karma was still in a fog, and the details of the surgery and the hours leading up to it were fuzzy. Part of her wanted to block that memory out. She felt a stinging pain in her insides, and her head throbbed.

"The baby will be in the NICU for a few weeks to strengthen his lungs. Otherwise, he appears to be in perfect health.

Karma smiled and looked at Jamal, who seemed distracted as he walked alongside her.

"I might throw up," said Karma, looking at Carla, suddenly nauseous.

Carla stopped the wheelchair. "Do you want us to return to your room? The anesthesia can do this to you."

"No! I want to see my baby now!" She started crying.

"Okay. We won't stay there long," Carla said, then resumed pushing her in the wheelchair.

"Did you see him?" Karma asked Jamal between her tears.

"Yeah. He's healthy," he said quietly, avoiding eye contact. Karma could smell his morning breath and noticed dark circles under his eyes. Even between her tears, she saw his wrinkled white shirt and disheveled hair. She had never seen him look that rough.

"We were so worried," Karma told the nurse, wiping her tears with the back of her hand. "He came so early; it was completely unexpected."

"Yeah. I've never seen a situation like this. Your baby is a very healthy preemie. It's like a miracle," she said. "We never expected him to survive. You were not even in your third trimester. The doctor is astounded."

Al Hamdulliah muttered Karma under her breath.

"The doctor is even considering writing about this case in a medical journal," the nurse chuckled.

Karma gave her a tired smile. He has always been special, all that kicking early on. My baby is mine. Both of us are different, freaks of nature.

"Who does he look like?" Karma asked, looking at Jamal.

"You'll see," he said, biting his lip.

Karma felt her heart drop to the floor. "What do you mean? Is there something wrong with him? What's wrong with my child?"

Jamal didn't respond.

When they took her to the incubator, she staggered out of her wheelchair. A sharp, searing pain sliced through her lower abdomen as she looked through the glass.

"That's not my child," she said, a look of confusion on her face.

Jamal let out a long sigh. "It is. They pulled him out of your womb. I saw the whole thing."

She looked again at the sleeping, red-haired infant with very pale, almost translucent skin. An image of Vadim flashed before her, followed by an image of Danielle smiling, showing her white teeth, and then Lilith with the black snake wrapped around her neck.

Karma gasped. "It can't be. He doesn't look like either of us. They must have mixed the babies. That's not my child. Where is my child?" She panicked.

"Is there a problem?" Carla asked, looking at the baby through the glass and then shifting her gaze to Karma.

"Where is my child? Where did you take him? Did you steal him, you ugly bitch?" shouted Karma, then grabbed Carla's arms.

"Calm down, calm down," Carla said quietly, removing Karma's grip. "That's him," she said, pointing at the baby.

"No, it's not," she snapped.

Jamal looked at the nurse and said, "Can you please give us a minute? She's just tired and hysterical."

Carla turned around and struck up a conversation with another nurse in the room.

How did this happen?

Did she have the red-hair gene in her DNA, or maybe that came from Jamal's side? It's not far-fetched. She knew some red-haired people in Bilaq.

A thought crossed her mind that made her shriek. Did sleeping with Vadim mess things up? It couldn't be. It wasn't scientifically possible.

Except Danielle said it was. The indigenous tribe.

Two fathers were better than one.

Karma felt very cold and started to shiver. The child opened his eyes, and she gasped.

He had the palest blue eyes she had ever seen. Lighter than the ocean, lighter than the sky. Lighter than a gas fire, lighter than a blue jay. Sinister eyes, the eyes of Satan himself, but that was not what made her shout.

It was his very dark, oval pupils.

"What's wrong with his eyes?" she asked, her lips quivering. "What's wrong with my baby's eyes?" she shrieked. She looked at Jamal, but he stayed silent. "What's wrong?" Carla asked, approaching the incubator, drawn by Karma's shouts.

"His eyes. There is something wrong with them," said Karma, who was now banging on the incubator.

Carla rolled her eyes and then let out a sigh. "Ma'am, if you don't calm down, we will have to sedate you. He can see fine. We checked him." Carla got closer to Karma and touched her face. "Are you okay, hon? You look very pale. We might have to take you back to your room. I don't want you to faint right here at the NICU."

Karma ignored her. "Why do his eyes look like this?"

The nurse looked down at the baby and was silent for a bit. "They're just unique. It happens. They'll probably normalize when he grows up. It also might be because he's a preemie."

"Why does my baby look like this?" she asked, tears welling in her eyes. "Can somebody tell me?"

Jamal squeezed her wrist so hard, almost crushing her bones. "Well, you tell me," he said.

She shrieked in pain.

Lilith, I need you. Come get me. Get me now.

Epilogue

KARMA CHECKED ON her one-year-old son. He was peacefully asleep in his crib. He was the sweetest baby. She never thought she would love anyone or anything as much as him. She kissed his forehead and went downstairs. Walking towards the dining room, she picked up the box, inspecting it for the second time. There was no return address, just as there was in last year's box. Inside were three worn-out journals with the same handwriting and the same person.

She was hesitant to open them.

What now? She thought. Does she really want to know? Does she really want to know what happened to that woman who shared her curse? How much did she fuck up her life? Is she even alive?

The doorbell rang, and then Baladi started barking. Karma worried that all that ruckus would wake up her son. Karma placed the box back on the table and waited a minute before walking to the front door, waiting to hear a baby's cry. Nothing. He was still sound asleep.

When she opened the door, there she was: Danielle.

"I need you," she said, then took a puff from her vape.

Karma glanced outside. Danielle's car was parked in her driveway, the same car she used to drive around to drop off groceries for those who had ordered them online, a job that made her mom happy.

"I can't now. The baby is asleep."

Danielle rolled her eyes. "Wake him up and bring him with us."

"Don't be cruel," said Karma. "He needs to rest; otherwise, he will be cranky all day."

"There's something fishy about this guy on Ott Street. I want you to look into it."

Karma crossed her arms and sighed. "Can you give me 30 minutes?"

"No, he might leave soon," she said, tapping her foot.

"Okay, okay, come on in. I need at least 10 minutes."

Karma went upstairs to grab her purse and then walked to the baby's room, gently tapping him. "Come on, sweety, we have to go. We have to stop the bad guys, you know. If we don't take care of them, they'll eat us alive. You and I can do anything."

The baby opened his eyes.

Karma smiled.